HEROES
REVEALED

HEROES

REVEALED
WRITTEN BY MICHAEL GOLDMAN

CONTENTS

FOREWORD

Welcome to *Heroes Revealed*!

This book is the first ever to carefully document the circuitous world of *Heroes* for our fans to enjoy. For the last few years, hundreds of extremely talented and dedicated people have been laboring to bring you this show each week, with a philosophy that we are, in a sense, speaking directly to you and taking creative inspiration directly from you. During this time, we have tried hard to actually be fans, to think like fans, and to design stories that would interest you in a graphic novel-style format that, while unique to television, is familiar and colorful.

Indeed, we launched the show at Comic-Con in 2006, and every year since, we bring our entire cast there to celebrate and interact with our fans. It was out of that unique slice of the pop culture world that this whole thing got rolling.

You fans are at the heart of that world—you understand our goal has always been to express deep themes that are particularly apropos these days. We wanted a show that promoted a global consciousness, in terms of storylines, cast, and locations. We wanted to tell archetypal stories about good and evil, with a unique visual style, and we wanted characters that were regular people when you strip away their special abilities—the cheerleader, the cop, the politician, the single mom, and so on. All of these ideas lent themselves to the vexing question—what would happen if these regular people had super powers? Abilities that could allow them to connect and work together for a greater good if, that is, they want it badly enough.

The overriding idea behind *Heroes* is the notion that we're all in this together. Only through finding and connecting with one another can we actually save the world, and even then, only if we make the choice to do so. From the beginning, the idea of free will was at the center of the story. We concluded that how you use your special power, if you use it at all, would likely depend on your nature and your circumstances. Might a good person use power for evil if they were destitute or grievously wronged? Would a criminal use power for good if given a new opportunity for redemption? Could they overcome their natural prejudices and limitations to achieve something greater?

These are the thematic constructs of *Heroes*. Even as we continue our story, moving from one chapter in this ongoing saga to the next, these questions will always be at the heart of what we are trying to do.

With all that said, I invite you to explore further what we've been up to in this comprehensive examination of our first three seasons. I hope you'll stay with us for the rest of the ride. Thanks!

Sincerely,

Tim Kring
Heroes creator/writer/producer

	1	2	3	4	5	6
A						
B						
C						
D						
E						

A-1 CLAIRE BENNET
POWER: RAPID CELL REGENERATION

A-2 NOAH BENNET

A-3 ELLE BISHOP
POWER: ELECTRICAL MANIPULATION

A-4 MONICA DAWSON
POWER: ADOPTIVE MUSCLE MEMORY

A-5 SIMONE DEVEAUX

A-6 D.L. HAWKINS
POWER: PHASING

A-7 MAYA HERRERA
POWER: POISON EMISSION

A-8 ANDO MASAHASHI

A-9 ISAAC MENDEZ
POWER: PRECOGNITION

A-10 ADAM MONROE
POWER: RAPID CELL REGENERATION

A-11 HIRO NAKAMURA
POWERS: SPACE/TIME
MANIPULATION

A-12 MATT PARKMAN
POWER: TELEPATHY

B-1 ANGELA PETRELLI
POWER: PRECOGNITIVE DREAMING

B-2 NATHAN PETRELLI
POWER: FLIGHT

B-3 PETER PETRELLI
POWER: EMPATHIC MIMICRY

B-4 MICAH SANDERS
POWER: TECHNOPATHY

B-5 NIKI SANDERS
POWER: SUPERHUMAN STRENGTH

B-6 TRACY STRAUSS
POWER: FREEZING

B-7 MOHINDER SURESH
GENETICIST

B-8 SYLAR/GABRIEL GRAY
POWER: INTUITIVE APTITUDE

B-9 BRIAN DAVIS
POWER: TELEKINESIS

B-10 DALE SMITHER
POWER: ENHANCED HEARING

B-11 ZANE TAYLOR
POWER: MELTING

B-12 CHARLIE ANDREWS
POWER: EIDETIC MEMORY

C-1 BOB BISHOP
POWER: ALCHEMY

C-2 CLAUDE RAINS
POWER: INVISIBILITY

C-3 HANA GITELMAN
POWER: CYBERPATHY

C-4 MEREDITH GORDON
POWER: PYROKINESIS

C-5 THE HAITIAN
POWERS: MEMORY REMOVAL
AND POWER DAMPENING

C-6 ALEJANDRO HERRERA
POWER: POISON NEGATION

C-7 SANJOG IYER
POWER: DREAM MANIPULATION

C-8 DANIEL LINDERMAN
POWER: HEALING

C-9 EDEN MCCAIN
POWER: VOCAL PERSUASION

C-10 KAITO NAKAMURA
POWER: PROBABILITY
COMPUTATION

C-11 MAURY PARKMAN
POWER: ADVANCED TELEPATHY

C-12 WEST ROSEN
POWER: FLIGHT

D-1 DAPHNE MILLBROOK
POWER: SUPERHUMAN SPEED

D-2 TED SPRAGUE
POWER: INDUCED RADIOACTIVITY

D-3 USUTU
POWER: PRECOGNITION

D-4 MOLLY WALKER
POWER: LOCATIONAL CLAIRVOYANCE

D-5 CANDICE WILMER
POWER: ILLUSION

D-6 ERIC DOYLE
PUPPETMASTER

D-7 THE GERMAN
POWER: MAGNETISM

D-8 KNOX WASHINGTON
POWER: SUPERHUMAN STRENGTH

D-9 FLINT GORDON
POWER: PYROKENSIS

D-10 JESSE MURPHY
POWER: SOUND MANIPULATION

D-11 CAITLIN

D-12 LYLE BENNET

E-1 SANDRA BENNET

E-2 NANA DAWSON

E-3 CHARLES DEVEAUX
POWER: RELATES TO DREAMS

E-4 JANICE PARKMAN

E-5 ARTHUR PETRELLI
POWER: POWER ABSORPTION

E-6 HEIDI PETRELLI

E-7 DR. CHANDRA SURESH
GENETICIST

E-8 AUDREY HANSON
FBI AGENT

E-9 THOMPSON

E-10 YAEKO
THE SWORDSMITH'S DAUGHTER

E-11 VICTORIA PRATT
GENETICIST

E-12 DR. ZIMMERMAN
GENETICIST

MOHINDER LABORS TO SOLVE THE RIDDLES OF HIS FATHER'S THEORIES, BUT CHANDRA LEFT BEHIND MORE THAN THEORIES—HE LEFT AN ALGORITHM TO LOCATE GENETICALLY SUPERIOR HUMANS.

"LEVITATION, TELEPORTATION, REGENERATION. IT IS NO LONGER SIMPLY A THEORY. I HAVE SEEN IT WITH MY OWN EYES."

PATIENT ZERO

Chandra's obsession unintentionally unleashes a horror on the world when he finally meets Patient Zero—watchmaker Gabriel Gray. He helps Gabriel find his talent, but pays for it with his life when Gabriel evolves in a way Chandra never expects—into the beast, Sylar.

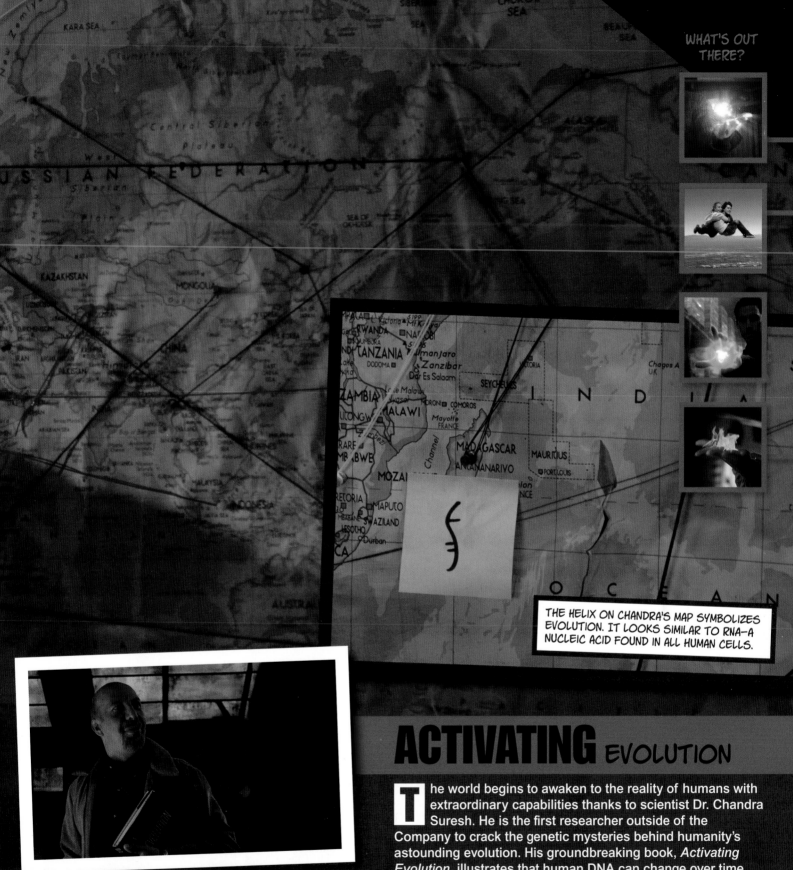

THE HELIX ON CHANDRA'S MAP SYMBOLIZES EVOLUTION. IT LOOKS SIMILAR TO RNA—A NUCLEIC ACID FOUND IN ALL HUMAN CELLS.

ACTIVATING EVOLUTION

The world begins to awaken to the reality of humans with extraordinary capabilities thanks to scientist Dr. Chandra Suresh. He is the first researcher outside of the Company to crack the genetic mysteries behind humanity's astounding evolution. His groundbreaking book, *Activating Evolution*, illustrates that human DNA can change over time, making advanced abilities like tissue regeneration, telepathy, and flight possible. Dr. Suresh also pioneers a mathematical theorem based on DNA migration patterns and data from the Human Genome Project to locate these individuals with special abilities, and he attempts to find thirty-six of them, including a primary target dubbed Patient Zero. Suresh is eventually murdered, but his research lives on through his son, Mohinder.

PIONEER

Geneticist Chandra Suresh gives up everything to pursue his obsession with evolution including, eventually, his life. He leaves his job and family in India, and moves to New York to continue his research, despite ridicule from his peers. His determination pays off when he locates Patient Zero, but, just as he is about to prove his theories correct, he is killed.

MOHINDER SURESH

Although not born with special abilities, Mohinder Suresh's life is dominated by his father Chandra's obsession with evolution. Eventually, he comes to share that obsession after his father dies and he confirms his theory that super-humans exist. As his research leads to confrontations with Sylar, entanglements with the Company, and relationships with genetically advanced people, Mohinder's obsession deepens until he gives himself synthetic abilities. Side effects, however, transform him into a monster, leading him to Pinehearst. There, he reverses his condition, but at a great price.

- **Power: Enhanced Senses (synthetically self-induced)**
- **Hometown: Madras, India; relocates to New York, NY**
- **Occupations: Genetics researcher and professor; Company agent; Pinehearst researcher; Cab driver**

Enhanced Senses
1. Through the injection of a synthetic formula, Mohinder acquires strength far in excess of a normal man, along with enhanced senses in all categories.
2. He mimics insect-like abilities to scale walls and stick to surfaces, and excretes a goo-like substance that can harden into a cocoon capable of holding human prey.
3. Side effects cover Mohinder's skin and body in reptilian scales and make him dangerously aggressive.

FATHER AND SON

Chandra Suresh's life work drives a wedge between him and his son, but eventually, it becomes Mohinder's life as well. For years, Mohinder feels his father's obsession, and lack of attention to his family, is deeply unfair. But after Chandra's murder, Mohinder learns why that work was so important.

"I TRIED TO STOP SYLAR. BUT I COULDN'T. I'M A SCIENTIST. I CAN'T FIGHT SOMEONE WHO DEFIED THE LAWS OF PHYSICS."

SANJOG IYER

Helping Mohinder unravel secrets of his father's research is a mysterious boy called Sanjog Iyer. He enters Mohinder's dreams and guides him in understanding his relationship with his father and also unlocking his research.

EDEN MCCAIN HELPS MOHINDER SEEK CLUES LEFT BEHIND BY HIS LATE FATHER IN HIS NEW YORK APARTMENT. POSING AS A FRIEND, SHE IS REALLY WORKING WITH THE COMPANY TO LOCATE CHANDRA'S DATA.

ALTHOUGH NOT NATURALLY ENHANCED HIMSELF, MOHINDER WAS BORN INTO A FAMILY DEEPLY IMPACTED BY HUMANITY'S EVOLUTIONARY MARCH.

MOHINDER IS OFTEN UNSURE WHICH SIDE TO TAKE IN THE WAR OVER HUMANITY'S FUTURE. CONSIDERING HIS RESEARCH THE PRIORITY, HE SOMETIMES SWITCHES SIDES.

"I WANT TO DO THE RIGHT THING HERE. FOR EVERYBODY."

SEEKING A CURE

Even after taking a broken nose from Niki Sanders, Mohinder's desire to rid her of the Shanti Virus is so strong that he joins the Company's plot to capture Claire Bennet in order to use her unique blood for a possible cure. He's so committed that, when things go wrong, he's willing to shoot Noah Bennet to save Bob Bishop and continue his research.

EVOLUTION GONE WRONG

Hidden in his lab at Isaac Mendez's old studio, an increasingly aggressive Mohinder Suresh begins to manufacture bizarre cocoons as his body continues to transform. Losing his sense of morality, he spins them to immobilize test subjects for his experiments on the genetic secrets behind his evolutionary misstep.

DESPERATION

As his transformation accelerates, so does Mohinder's willingness to experiment with a possible cure. At Pinehearst, at Arthur Petrelli's urging, he injects it into test subjects, sometimes with ghastly results. Finally, Arthur is able to supply the key to perfecting the Formula—a Catalyst secretly kept by the Nakamura family.

AMONG THE MANY OTHERS INTERESTED IN MOHINDER'S WORK IS SYLAR, WHO DECEIVES HIM BY PRETENDING TO BE AN EVOLVED HUMAN NAMED ZANE TAYLOR IN ORDER TO GAIN ACCESS TO THE LIST OF SUPER-POWERED INDIVIDUALS.

AS PETER PETRELLI ENTERS MOHINDER'S APARTMENT, HE DOESN'T REALIZE THE SCIENTIST IS TELEKINETICALLY PINNED TO THE CEILING ABOVE HIM—THE WORK OF SYLAR, WHO WILL MOMENTARILY INITIATE HIS FIRST CONFRONTATION WITH PETER.

THE FOUNDERS

Each of the founders is a genetically advanced human except, possibly, for Victoria Pratt. They all originally shared a desire to improve the world, but they do not always agree on what that entails. This photo was taken at their last known gathering. **1. SUSAN AMMAN** Records reveal nothing about her other than that she is a Company founder, and is believed dead. **2. DANIEL LINDERMAN** joins forces with his Vietnam comrade, Arthur Petrelli, after the war to form the Company's nucleus and runs the operation until his death. *Power: Healing.* **3. ARTHUR PETRELLI** Incredibly powerful, Petrelli's cold-blooded nature leads to his apparent death. He resurfaces, however, with a new

organization and a dark agenda. *Power: Power Absorption.* **4. ANGELA PETRELLI** steadfastly supports the Company. After the deaths of Linderman and Bishop, she takes over. *Power: Precognitive Dreaming.* **5. KAITO NAKAMURA** Although hard-edged, he is a tireless believer in the original mission to do good, but he is silenced by Adam Monroe. *Power: Probability Computation.* **6. BOB BISHOP** The organization's longtime financier, Bishop takes over as Company head upon Linderman's death and proves particularly ruthless before falling victim to Sylar. *Power: Alchemy.* **7. VICTORIA PRATT** To her horror, she engineers the deadly form of the Shanti Virus, leading to her

demise. **8. MAURY PARKMAN** A powerful telepath, Parkman abandons his family to serve the Company, but years later is killed by Arthur while protecting his son. *Power: Advanced Telepathy.* **9. PAULA GRAMBLE** appears on Chandra Suresh's list of evolved humans, but her fate is unknown. **10. CHARLES DEVEAUX** The most committed to the original altruistic ideals of the Company, Deveaux dies peacefully in his seventies. *Power: is related to dreams.* **11. CARLOS MENDEZ** Largely unknown, he is believed to be deceased, and some suspect he is Isaac Mendez's father. **12. HARRY FLETCHER** All that is known about Fletcher is that he is on Chandra's list and is believed dead.

In 1977, twelve individuals aware of genetically evolved humans unite at the behest of a man named Adam Monroe and form a covert organization named the Company. They aim to use their special abilities to find, protect, and when necessary control others with advanced powers. Monroe approaches two Vietnam War veterans—Arthur Petrelli and Daniel Linderman—and Japanese industrialist Kaito Nakamura to launch the operation, and they recruit nine other believers in the cause, including key figures like Petrelli's wife, Angela, businessman Charles Deveaux, con-man Maury Parkman, and geneticist Victoria Pratt.

"THE WORLD IS BROKEN. IT NEEDS A FRESH START."

DEATH THREATS

Seeking revenge for his incarceration, Adam sets out to kill the remaining founders. He sends them pieces of their original group photo, marked with the threatening Helix symbol. He succeeds with Kaito Nakamura, but fails to kill Angela Petrelli.

FOUNDER KILLED

NYPD Detective Matt Parkman investigates the murder of Kaito Nakamura, who plummeted to his death from the rooftop of the Deveaux Building.

INTERROGATION

Determined to solve the mystery of the death threats, Matt interrogates Angela Petrelli, who is equally determined not to reveal how the Company connects all the victims.

ADAM PINES FOR A WORLD DOMINATED BY THE GENETICALLY GIFTED AND IS WILLING TO COMMIT MASS MURDER TO ACHIEVE IT. WHEN THIS AGENDA BECOMES CLEAR, HIS COLLEAGUES IMPRISON HIM.

ANOTHER VICTIM

By manipulating Peter Petrelli, Adam causes the death of another Company founder, a person with important information about a deadly virus—Victoria Pratt.

DANIEL LINDERMAN

Infamous businessman Linderman is a living contradiction—able to cure the sick, he's willing to kill millions. Serving as an idealistic medic in Vietnam, a secret mission teaches him to accept that sometimes harsh action is required to achieve complex goals. This lesson leads him onto a winding path. Seeking to make humanity safer, he co-founds the Company, but becomes frustrated at saving only one person at a time, and so justifies a plan to commit mass murder to supposedly cleanse a sick world. Ultimately, his exploitation of people in pursuit of this twisted agenda leads to his own violent death.

- **Power: Healing**
- **Hometown: Denver, CO; relocates to Las Vegas, NV**
- **Occupations: Founder of the Linderman Group and suspected crime baron; Co-founder and Director of the Company**

Healing
1. The ability to instantly cure injury and illness in other living things, returning them to sound health regardless of the trauma's severity, short of death.
2. Health is restored to humans, animals, and plants through the slightest touch.

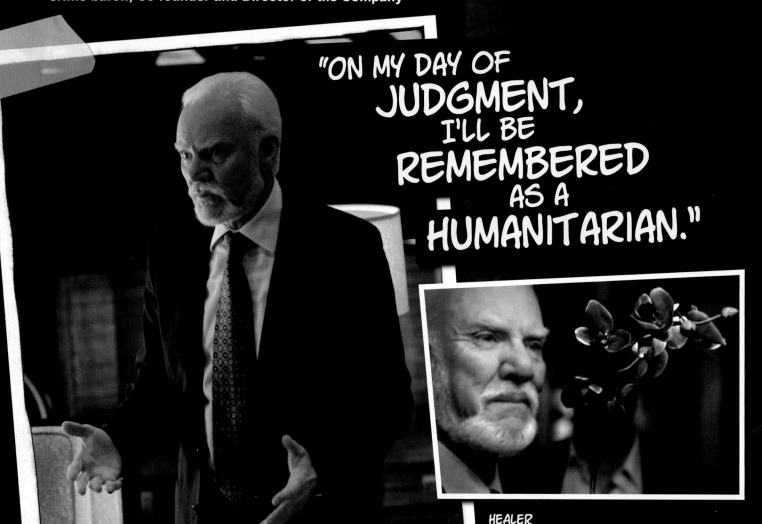

"ON MY DAY OF **JUDGMENT**, I'LL BE **REMEMBERED** AS A **HUMANITARIAN.**"

THE WORLD CONSIDERS LINDERMAN A RUTHLESS BUSINESSMAN AND CRIME FIGURE, BUT HE SEES HIMSELF AS THE SAVIOR OF HUMANITY.

HEALER
When Nathan Petrelli rhetorically asks Linderman what he knows about healing, he reveals his power and the dichotomy of his existence by reviving a dying flower.

NIKI SANDERS FINDS HER LIFE CONSUMED BY LINDERMAN. SHE HAS WORKED FOR HIM, BEEN THREATENED BY HIM, AND SEEN HER HUSBAND AND SON FORCED DEEP INTO HIS WEB.

BEYOND DEATH

Linderman instructs Daphne Millbrook to bring Matt Parkman and other recruits to Arthur Petrelli's organization—an amazing feat considering Linderman is dead. In fact, this Linderman is just a detailed hallucination, planted into Daphne's mind by Maury Parkman on orders from Arthur Petrelli.

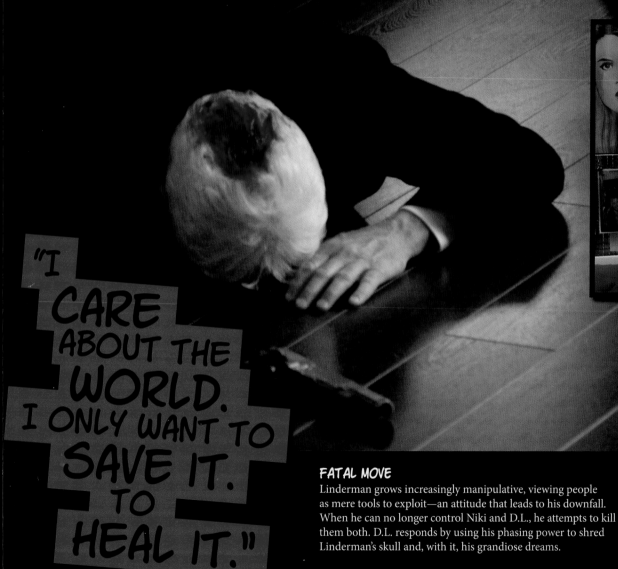

"I CARE ABOUT THE WORLD. I ONLY WANT TO SAVE IT. TO HEAL IT."

FATAL MOVE

Linderman grows increasingly manipulative, viewing people as mere tools to exploit—an attitude that leads to his downfall. When he can no longer control Niki and D.L., he attempts to kill them both. D.L. responds by using his phasing power to shred Linderman's skull and, with it, his grandiose dreams.

MANIPULATION

Seeking to rescue their son Micah from Linderman, Niki and D.L. break into his inner sanctum. To their horror, they find evidence that shows their entire relationship —even their son's birth—has been covertly orchestrated by Linderman. Papers, photos, and sensitive data illustrate the extent of the family's manipulation.

DESPITE LINDERMAN'S EFFORTS TO GIVE HIM GREAT POWER, POLITICIAN NATHAN PETRELLI RESISTS BEING A PUPPET. MAURY PARKMAN, HOWEVER, LATER PLANTS INFLUENCING HALLUCINATIONS OF LINDERMAN IN NATHAN'S VULNERABLE MIND.

MICAH SANDERS IS FORCED TO USE HIS POWER TO HELP LINDERMAN RIG NATHAN'S CONGRESSIONAL VICTORY. HOWEVER, NIKI AND D.L. WILL SEEK REVENGE AGAINST LINDERMAN FOR ENDANGERING MICAH.

ANGELA PETRELLI

Angela Petrelli spearheads Company conspiracies—such as a mass murder plot, the exploitation of her own children, and the emotional manipulation of a cold-blooded killer—all in the name of what she calls the greater good. She is a contradiction—willing, on the one hand, to subordinate her children's welfare to the plan to destroy New York, and yet, in other circumstances, proving deadly calculating to protect them, as her husband Arthur learns to his detriment. When Arthur resurfaces, Angela is forced to re-evaluate her position in the struggle for humanity's future.

- **Power: Precognitive Dreaming**
- **Hometown: New York City, NY**
- **Occupations: Major shareholder in Yamagato Industries; Co-founder and later Director of Operations of the Company**

Precognitive Dreaming
1. The ability to see specific future events while dreaming in a deep state of REM sleep.
2. The meaning or details of those events are not always clear, and are subject to interpretation.

THE PETRELLI FAMILY MATRIARCH CAN BE RUTHLESS, MANIPULATIVE, AND CAPABLE OF GREAT MORAL COMPROMISES.

"I'VE DONE SO MANY BAD THINGS. IT DOESN'T MATTER WHAT CRIME I'M CONFESSING TO."

FIRST BORN
Angela's relationship with her eldest son, Nathan, is terribly complicated. She apparently permitted the manipulation of his DNA to give him a synthetic super power, and participated in a conspiracy to make him President. Yet, though she has high hopes for Nathan, she routinely enrages him with her tactics. Ironically, Nathan later pursues his own dark agenda, using the same justification Angela has always used—namely, that he is trying to protect the world.

FAVORITE SON
While viewing Nathan as a strong, natural leader, Angela tries to protect Peter, feeling he is more vulnerable and sensitive, and treats him as her favorite over the years. She agonizes by Peter's side when he is comatose and mourns when he appears dead, but the Company agenda comes first, and she is more than willing to set aside her concern for him during the Kirby Plaza affair to, from her perspective, save humanity.

"I AM BETTER. IT'S NOT A BELIEF, IT'S A FACT."

IN CONTROL
Despite complete paralysis, Arthur Petrelli remains in firm control. His body no longer works, but his mind remains active, allowing him to communicate telepathically and use his power. He thus assembles his team, and gets their help in regaining his health. He has Adam Monroe kidnapped, and steals his regenerative power —instantly restoring his body.

VILLAINS
Petrelli establishes Pinehearst Company to achieve evolutionary dominance. He assembles, and frequently manipulates, a team of villains. Among them are Sylar, Elle Bishop, Flint Gordon, Tracy Strauss, and Knox.

ARTHUR PETRELLI

Since his violent time in Vietnam, Arthur Petrelli has been steadfastly destroying people to fulfill a grandiose agenda, even after co-founding the Company. His goal: to create a world ruled by genetically advanced people, with himself at the helm. He suffers a major setback when his wife learns of his treachery and almost kills him, but his power allows him to secretly survive, paralyzed. He returns with a vengeance—assembling a team of super-powered villains to aid his plan to redevelop the Formula capable of creating a race of super-powered humans. Ironically, the Formula works, but Arthur never lives to see it as Sylar deals him the ultimate punishment.

- **Power: Power Absorption**
- **Hometown: New York City, NY**
- **Occupation: Former US Army Special Ops Soldier; Criminal defense attorney; Co-founder of the Company; Founder of Pinehearst**

PETRELLI WON'T LET MORALITY, OPPOSITION, OR DEATH STOP HIM.

Power Absorption
1. The ability to instantly steal—rather than mimic—the abilities of other genetically advanced people through brief physical contact, leaving the victim permanently wiped clean of their power.
2. The process causes great pain, but does not normally kill the victim. An exception to this is Adam Monroe, who without his power was 400 years old.

KAITO NAKAMURA

Business magnate Kaito Nakamura built his life around traditional Japanese values such as honor and duty, but the reality of his own special abilities forced him into a morally gray world. His role as a founding member of the Company becomes increasingly perverted by the organization's aggressive pursuit of what it considers a greater good. When his talent for predicting situational outcomes helps him realize his death is looming, Nakamura seeks redemption by supporting his son, Hiro, in his mission to "save the world."

- **Power:** Probability Computation
- **Hometown:** Tokyo, Japan
- **Occupations:** CEO of Yamagato Industries; Co-founder of the Company

Probability Computation

1. The ability to instantly analyze statistical probabilities, and compute likely outcomes—a skill that helped Nakamura become a Japanese captain of industry.

FATHER AND SON

Kaito believes the Nakamuras have a destiny to help the world, but he never thought his son, Hiro, would amount to much. It takes nearly 30 years for father and son to connect, but when they do, Kaito tests Hiro's resolve and skills, and pronounces him ready for his journey.

HE MAY APPEAR A STUFFY BUSINESSMAN, BOUND BY RIGID SOCIAL VALUES, BUT KAITO IS A HERO WHO STRIVES TO SAVE THE WORLD.

FORESHADOW

Kaito Nakamura's fate—murder at the hands of his immortal enemy, Adam Monroe—is foretold in an eerie Isaac Mendez painting. Kaito's ability to calculate the likely outcomes of his various options enables him to stoically accept his fate, even when Hiro attempts to use his time-travel abilities to help him cheat death.

"WE HAVE THE POWER OF GODS. THAT DOES NOT MEAN WE CAN PLAY GOD."

FATHER AND DAUGHTER

Bishop ruthlessly trains his daughter, Elle, to work as a Company operative, denying her a normal childhood, and yet, when she is wounded, he is clearly concerned for her welfare. He makes the Company the center of Elle's existence; whether this is to protect her from becoming a target, or out of service to the Company is not clear. It also isn't known whether she was placed in Bishop's home by the Company, like Claire in the Bennet household.

> FOR 30 YEARS, BISHOP BANK-ROLLED COMPANY OPERATIONS.

COMPANY MAN

Bob Bishop is ruthless, but not cowardly. He stays at Primatech in the face of an expected infiltration by Maury Parkman, who is acting under orders to assassinate him. Bishop also remains at his post knowing Sylar is loose—a decision that results in his murder at Sylar's hands.

BOB BISHOP

Bob Bishop is the quintessential, unwavering believer in the Company's mission and he willingly embraces the moral compromises surrounding it. A founding member of the Company, Bishop uses his alchemy power to finance the organization, and upon the death of Linderman, he takes over the supervision of day-to-day operations, exhibiting a growing ruthless streak. Bishop routinely places his daughter, Elle, in danger and relentlessly pushes her to be as callous as he is.

"TRUST ME. IT'S EASIER TO ASK FORGIVENESS THAN PERMISSION."

Alchemy
1. The transmutation of the molecular composition of base metals, and possibly other substances, into gold.

- ■ **Power:** Alchemy
- ■ **Base of Operations:** Hartsdale, New York
- ■ **Occupation:** Regional Sales Manager, Primatech; Director of Operations, the Company

THE NIGHTMARE MAN:
MAURY PARKMAN CAN MAKE
YOU BELIEVE WHATEVER HE
WANTS YOU TO BELIEVE.

CONFRONTATION

As skillful at deceit as he is at mind manipulation, Maury Parkman feigns surprise when confronted by his son, Matt, and Nathan Petrelli. He pulls a gun, claiming he's been threatened like the other Company founders. But it's a ruse as he prepares to strike with his real weapon—mental telepathy.

"IT WAS A TEMPTATION. I WAS WEAK. I USED PEOPLE. I WAS AWFUL."

MANIPULATION

Reality slips away from a distraught Niki Sanders as Parkman alters her perceptions during his strike against Bob Bishop. He seems responsible for the assassinations of his fellow Company founders, but in reality, he's a human weapon, serving Adam Monroe.

MAURY PARKMAN

Maury Parkman lost his idealism and moral center long ago, and has been using his power for personal gain for decades. Even the return of Matt, the son he abandoned, fails to awaken his sense of decency, and a confrontation between father and son results. Matt imprisons Maury in his own worst nightmare, but with Maury, things often aren't what they seem. Presumed incapacitated, he soon turns up helping Arthur Petrelli recruit evolved humans for Pinehearst. Ironically, challenging Arthur over his son's welfare proves to be Maury's fatal error.

■ **Power:** Advanced Telepathy
■ **Hometown:** Philadelphia, PA
■ **Occupations:** Petty thief; Co-founder of the Company

Advanced Telepathy
1. The ability to read minds, and communicate thoughts and feelings to others without using speech, writing, or touch.
2. Maury is capable of trapping individuals in detailed hallucinations built out of a victim's memories.
3. He is able to incapacitate or cause victims great pain by shutting down portions of their brain.

CHARLES DEVEAUX

While some of the founders of the Company lose sight of their original mission to use their gifts to pursue greater good in the world, Charles Deveaux never does. Even with his dying breath, he argues that an optimistic future is possible, and that those pure of heart are best suited to realizing it. Specifically, he intuitively recognizes such qualities in Peter Petrelli and foreshadows the role Peter will soon play in changing the world. His ability to communicate support to Peter across time, space, and different states of consciousness is central to Peter's acceptance of his burdensome role.

- **Power:** Unclear, related to communication via dreams
- **Hometown:** New York, NY
- **Occupations:** Businessman; Co-founder of the Company

The exact nature of Charles Deveaux's powers is unclear. His encounters with Peter Petrelli indicate he has the ability to interact with other individuals in or through their dreams, but that has not been officially confirmed.

EVEN IN THE FACE OF DEATH, CHARLES REMAINS OPTIMISTIC ABOUT HUMANKIND.

"IN THE END, IT'S ONLY LOVE THAT MATTERS."

UNIQUE ENCOUNTER

However his special skill might be defined or explained, Charles Deveaux utilizes it during an encounter with a dreaming Peter Petrelli on the rooftop of the Deveaux Building. In his dream, Peter watches his mother, Angela, discuss plans with Deveaux for healing the world after the coming, and seemingly inevitable, destruction of New York. Deveaux then detects the presence of the other-worldly Peter and speaks to him in his dream. Charles' words and presence reassure Peter, and leave him profoundly moved.

SIMONE DEVEAUX

Art dealer Simone Deveaux brings her father together with Peter Petrelli by hiring Peter as Charles' caregiver during the final days of his illness. Along the way, despite her troubled relationship with the painter Isaac Mendez, she falls in love with Peter. That reality makes her demise even more tragic—she's accidentally shot dead by Isaac in a fit of rage directed at Peter.

THE COMPANY

The covert organization known only as "the Company" has evolved dramatically since it began in 1977. Founded by 12 apparently well-intentioned people, its purpose was to [us]e special skills to better the world. However, the founders [be]came divided over the best way to fulfill this mission and [wh]ether they should use their powers to play God. Many [bel]ieve the organization has lost its way thanks to dangerous [pro]jects such as the Shanti virus and synthetic abilities. Basic [pra]ctices include finding and protecting evolved humans, while [elimi]nating those considered dangerous. Its use of two-agent [tea]ms (one agent evolved, one genetically standard), charged [wit]h "bagging and tagging" people for monitoring purposes [has] led to violent retaliatory strikes. The Company operates [an]d outside the law, kidnaps and ruthlessly tests people, wipes [me]mories, and even executes those it considers harmful.

A VERY ORDINARY PAPER COMPANY

For decades, the Company's primary headquarters in Odessa, Texas, has hidden behind a front company called the Primatech Paper Company. Primatech's website claims it has been "manufacturing and distributing high-quality paper products since 1962," and the facility's entire first level is, in fact, a functional paper factory. However, its lower levels make up the Company's nerve center, and most of Primatech's top executives over the years have been, in reality, senior-level Company officials.

THOMPSON

Mr. Thompson functions as a mid-level Company manager supervising, among others, Noah Bennet, whom he originally recruited to the Company. When Bennet turns on the Company and attempts to terminate the Walker Tracking System, he shoots Thompson for trying to stop him. Thompson's legacy at the Company continues in the person of his son, field agent Eric Thompson.

BOB BISHOP

Bob Bishop, one of the founders of the Company, has assisted in the running and funding of its operations for many years, and takes over command upon Linderman's death. He operates ruthlessly until Sylar infiltrates the Company and brutally kills him.

DANIEL LINDERMAN

Another Company founder, Daniel Linderman, runs the organization from behind the scenes, while posing as a wealthy Las Vegas mobster. He is a driving force in its growing ruthless nature, and is even willing to let an entire city be destroyed to further the organization's agenda.

"WE FIND PEOPLE AND WE MAKE SURE THEY DON'T BECOME DANGEROUS."

ANGELA PETRELLI

Company co-founder Angela Petrelli functions secretively for years before eventually taking charge. She assists Linderman's conspiracy, moves to reign in Sylar, and eventually faces off with the man she thought was dead—her husband Arthur Petrelli.

PNEUMATIC SYRINGE

This modified medical device injects radioisotopes into evolved humans so the Company can locate them using a tracking satellite.

PNEUMATIC SYRINGE- ASSEMBLY DIAGRAM

WARNING
The material in this document is proprietary. Unauthorized distribution will result in severe criminal penalties.

"BAGGED AND TAGGED"

Individuals injected by the pneumatic syringe are all left with this tell-tale mark on their necks.

LEVEL 5

The most dangerous specially powered humans captured by the Company are normally held in the detention area known as Level 5—a sophisticated prison facility located deep underneath the main Primatech building. Cells on Level 5 are designed to neutralize the special abilities of their occupants, including Benjamin "Knox" Washington (pictured)—a member of the largest and most dangerous group of Level 5 prisoners to ever escape the facility.

NOAH BENNET

Noah Bennet—known to some as the "Man with the Horn-rimmed Glasses"—lives two lives, with contrasting moral codes. To the outside world he is a suburban husband and father in a boring job, but in fact he has been secretly in the employ of the Company for years. However, when his daughter, Claire is threatened, he doesn't hesitate in putting his family first and he turns on the Company. But even after this, Noah refuses to sit out the war over humanity's future, and has apparently joined a government program to control evolved humans. Noah's exact agenda, however, remains a mystery.

- **Power: No genetically evolved powers**
- **Hometown: Odessa, TX; Costa Verde, CA; New York City, NY**
- **Occupation: Company agent, trainer, and supervisor with cover jobs at Primatech Paper Company and Copy Kingdom**

NOAH BENNET IS CONFLICTED—HE FEARS UNCHECKED EVOLUTION, BUT ALSO WORKS WITH, AND PROTECTS, MANY EVOLVED HUMANS.

Bag and Tag
1. Company agents conduct "bag and tag" missions, where evolved humans are captured, tested, and injected with radioisotopes for monitoring purposes.
2. Bag and tag teams consist of a highly trained agent with no special abilities and an agent with powers. All but the most dangerous subjects are released, their memories of the experience wiped by the Haitian.

FAMILY BOND
For years, Noah Bennet's wife, Sandra, and son, Lyle, live a routine life—she raises show dogs and Lyle attends high school just like anyone else. When the truth about Noah and Claire is finally revealed, their lives are turned upside down. Although this stretches their bond, it won't break—they remain loyal to Noah and do what they can to help him.

"I'M COMFORTABLE WITH MORALLY GRAY."

TYPICAL OF NOAH'S MORAL AMBIGUITY, HE IS WILLING TO GIVE ISAAC MENDEZ HEROIN IF THAT'S WHAT IT TAKES TO TRIGGER HIS PREGONITIVE POWER.

"I THOUGHT WE WERE DOING GOOD. SAVING THE WORLD."

PARTNERS

Noah's Company partner is the Haitian. They make a formidable bag and tag team, taking down people with frightening abilities. They are to remain so close that the Haitian will aid Noah's efforts to escape the Company and launch a plan to destroy it.

COMPLEX RELATIONS

Since literally being forced to adopt Claire, Noah has tried to protect her by reluctantly deceiving her about his real life, and hers. It's almost a relief when the truth finally comes out, and he realizes Claire is capable of protecting herself and possesses more courage than anyone he's ever known.

ENEMY

Noah routinely intersects with the world's most dangerous people, including Sylar, who becomes Noah's mortal enemy. Noah obeys Company orders to keep him alive, and that decision costs him a good agent—Eden McCain. Months later, Noah will be forced to work briefly with Sylar, but he continues scheming to kill him.

TO HELP CLAIRE ESCAPE THE COMPANY'S WEB, NOAH INSTRUCTS THE HAITIAN TO WIPE HIS MIND OF HER WHEREABOUTS AND THEN SHOOT HIM TO MAKE HER STAGED ESCAPE LOOK REAL.

AFTER FORCING VALUABLE INFORMATION FROM HIM, NOAH COLDLY MURDERS HIS COMPANY MENTOR—IVAN SPEKTOR, THE MAN WHO TRAINED HIM—TO ENSURE THE COMPANY WILL

THE HAITIAN

The Haitian comes to the Company's attention at a young age after manifesting in his home country. Possessing a valuable ability, he is brought to the United States where he is trained as a Company agent and becomes a crucial asset, helping to bag and tag targets for years. He chooses to be a silent, passive presence most of the time, but this approach helps him periodically deviate from protocol when he sees fit, such as helping Noah Bennet protect his daughter, and letting Peter Petrelli escape. Events, including a Shanti Virus bout, the Arthur Petrelli affair, and unfinished family business in Haiti periodically force him to the forefront.

- **Power: Memory Removal and Power Dampening**
- **Home: 25 miles from Port-Au-Prince, Haiti; relocates to Odessa, TX**
- **Occupation: Longtime Company operative**

Memory Removal
1. The ability to erase memories from a person's mind merely by touch.
2. It is extremely precise—he can remove just certain memories, memories from particular time periods, or memories on particular subjects.

Power Dampening
1. The ability to temporarily block the special abilities of any genetically evolved person in his presence for as long as they remain in proximity.

"I CAN MAKE YOU FORGET IT ALL IF THAT'S WHAT YOU WOULD PREFER."

REMOVING MEMORY STRANDS

When the Haitian is first brought to the Company by Mr. Thompson, he refuses to speak. Asked about his power, he draws a picture of himself pulling what look like worms out of a person's head. This is how he removes selected strands of memory—using just hand touch and delicate concentration.

BLUNT FORCE

The Haitian's second ability allows Noah Bennet and others to deal with incredibly powerful subjects on an equal footing and in safety, as long as the Haitian is present. Blunting Eden McCain's power of persuasion, he leaves her no choice but to listen to the deal Noah Bennet offers: work for the Company or face imprisonment.

FOR YEARS, THE HAITIAN PARTNERS WITH NOAH BENNET. ONE OF HIS EARLIEST TASKS IS TO WIPE SANDRA BENNET'S MIND WHEN SHE LEARNS COMPANY BUSINESS—IT'S NOT THE ONLY TIME THIS WILL HAPPEN.

CAST OUT BY HIS VILLAGE BACK HOME AFTER HIS ABILITY SURFACES AND INADVERTENTLY HARMS HIS POWERFUL FATHER, THE HAITIAN FINDS NEW PURPOSE WITH THE COMPANY.

CHILDHOOD TRAGEDY

As a child, the Haitian idolizes his father, Guillame, who is known as the Houngan—a prominent spiritual leader of his people thanks to his ability to plant "bliss and horror" into minds. One tragic day, the Haitian's power manifests, and he unwittingly blunts his father's powers, preventing him from protecting his village from the brutal private militia known as the Tonton Macoutes. Having failed his people, Guillame blames his son and eventually decides to kill him. However, the boy's ability helps Guillame realize he has lost his way, as in a mythical story he tells his son about the snake and the crane. Guillame decides to kill himself instead, leaving a lasting mark on his son.

"WHAT **YOU** CAN DO... WHAT **I** CAN DO... THAT IS **GOD**. RESPECT IT ACCORDINGLY."

THE HAITIAN RETURNS HOME, WITH HELP FROM THE PETRELLIS, TO CONFRONT HIS BROTHER, SAMEDI, A BRUTAL LEVEL 5 ESCAPEE WITH DIAMOND-HARD SKIN. SAMEDI'S MILITIA KILLS PEOPLE AND KIDNAPS GIRLS, SELLING THEM INTO SLAVERY. THE BROTHERS FACE OFF, AND THE EVENT ILLUMINATES THE GROWING DIVIDE BETWEEN THE PETRELLI BROTHERS.

NOAH ORDERS THE HAITIAN TO REMOVE CLAIRE BENNET'S KNOWLEDGE OF OTHER SUPER-POWERED HUMANS AND HER FATHER'S INVOLVEMENT WITH THEM. BUT THE HAITIAN DOESN'T COMPLY—HE TELLS CLAIRE TO PRETEND SHE DOESN'T KNOW.

THE COMPANY TASKS THE HAITIAN WITH BRINGING PETER PETRELLI BACK AFTER HE ESCAPES. HOWEVER, AT ANGELA PETRELLI'S BEHEST, HE INSTEAD WIPES PETER'S MEMORY AND ARRANGES FOR HIM TO SLIP AWAY TO IRELAND.

the DEVEAUX ROOFTOP

The Deveaux Building on Central Park West is named after the billionnaire industrialist Charles Deveaux. Before his death, he lived in its penthouse and enjoyed this rooftop terrace, a place that plays a recurring role in the events surrounding those with powers. It is where baby Claire is given to Noah Bennet, where Peter Petrelli visits Charles in his dreams, where Claude Rains tends his pigeons, and where Katio Nakamura is pushed to his death. Precognitive Isaac Mendez paints these ornate rooftop designs against an ominous skyline. In this apocalyptic future, New York City is burning. His painting is a harbinger of what may well come to pass, unless Isaac and other Heroes can figure out a way to stop it.

HIRO NAKAMURA

Due to his positive nature, humor, and sense of justice, Hiro Nakamura is perhaps the most uncorrupted of all evolved humans. Determined to help others, he embarks on a journey to find other heroes and save New York. When his time journey to Feudal Japan unleashes a menace, Hiro labors to make things right, and he does so again to stop Arthur Petrelli. Even when he loses two ill-fated romances, and even when Arthur takes his power, Hiro maintains his upbeat view of life.

- **Power: Space/Time Manipulation**
- **Hometown: Tokyo, Japan**
- **Occupations: Programmer and then CEO, Yamagato Industries; views primary occupation as "superhero"**

Space/Time Manipulation
1. The ability to alter the space-time continuum in order to slow time and interact freely with people and objects that are "frozen."
2. The ability to teleport across long distances and backwards and forwards in time instantly—essentially folding space to reach his destination.
3. He can teleport or time-travel with one or more other people by having physical contact with them.

"NEW YORK CITY! I TELEPORTED HERE!"

YATTA!

A jubilant Hiro screams the Japanese word for "I did it!" as he suddenly finds himself in New York's Times Square—teleporting successfully for the first time using concentration. He won't have much time to celebrate, however, as the event starts a dangerous adventure.

FUTURE HIRO

Hiro's adventures continue in the future without his joyful spirit. Future Hiro is branded a terrorist for opposing an oppressive government. His dark disposition reflects the loss of his friend, Ando, who was killed in this timeline. His present-day self, however, gives this Hiro a chance to right wrongs.

EARLY IN THEIR MISSION, HIRO MOMENTARILY FALTERS WHEN ANDO CONVINCES HIM, AGAINST HIS BETTER JUDGMENT, TO USE HIS SPECIAL POWER TO EARN THEM SOME CASH IN THE CORINTHIAN CASINO IN LAS VEGAS.

SOME MIGHT CONSIDER HIM A HAPPY-GO-LUCKY POP-CULTURE GEEK, BUT HIRO NAKAMURA TAKES THE THEMES HE LEARNED GROWING UP—HONOR, JUSTICE, HEROISM—VERY SERIOUSLY.

MYSTICAL SWORD
An Isaac Mendez painting convinces Hiro he can be as heroic as Japanese legend, Takezo Kensei, if only he can acquire Kensei's legendary sword, so he schemes to steal it from the New York Museum of Natural History. It's a fake, however, and so, Hiro pursues the real sword all the way to Daniel Linderman's lair.

"A HERO DOES NOT RUN AWAY FROM HIS DESTINY."

FAVORITE PLACE
Ando, struggling to get through to Hiro while he has the mind of a 10-year-old, suggests he teleport them to a familiar place, and so, the "young" Hiro transports them to a Tokyo comic book shop. Ando is exasperated, but soon discovers the store holds the answer they need, in Isaac Mendez's prophetic *9th Wonders!* comic book.

ISAAC MENDEZ'S PAINTING OF HIRO AND ANDO BENEATH A BLOOD-SOAKED HOMECOMING BANNER HELPS CONVINCE THEM OF THE NEED TO SAVE THE CHEERLEADER AT ALL COSTS.

HIRO AT FIRST REFUSES TO EULOGIZE HIS FATHER, UNABLE TO ACCEPT HIS DEATH. USING HIS POWER TO TRY AND SAVE HIM, HE LEARNS THAT NOT EVEN HE CAN DENY DESTINY.

HIRO and the DINOSAUR

Isaac Mendez's painting of Hiro Nakamura's quest for the legendary sword of Takezo Kensei—the first he paints drug-free—is accurate but misleading. Hiro's fears about stepping on a prehistoric bug and changing history are, at least in this case, unfounded because he never travels to prehistoric times to battle an actual Tyrannosaurus Rex. In reality, the image comes from a present-day moment in which Hiro playfully taunts a model of a giant dinosaur at the New York City Museum of Natural History. He goes there to steal the sword, only to discover that it's a fake, placed there "courtesy of the Linderman Group." In order to retrieve the real sword—and hopefully restore his powers in the process—Hiro must infiltrate the private art collection of the infamous Mafia boss, Daniel Linderman.

TO BE A HIRO

Since the first time he blinked his eyes and stopped time, Hiro Nakamura has traveled an amazing path. An office drone one day, he battles the world's most dangerous villains and moves through time to meet his childhood hero the next. Having little experience with women, he nevertheless charms two beauties in the past he can never have in the present. After failing to impress his father for years, he eventually earns his legacy. A grown man, he experiences the wonder of childhood again. Lost in heroic fantasies, Hiro eventually becomes the personification of those fantasies—a true hero, working for good.

DRONE

Even as a simple office worker, Hiro Nakamura believes he has unique abilities. For months, he tries to stop a clock in his cubicle, with no success. Even his closest friend, Ando, thinks he's only fantasizing.

MANIFESTATION

One day, following the great eclipse, Hiro squints and concentrates, and all of a sudden, he succeeds—the clock stops for a second, and his life changes. Soon after, he focuses on a poster of New York, and suddenly—inexplicably—he's there.

LEARNING PHASE

Hiro's skill, at first, seems like a game to him—he uses it frivolously to make a train late and sneak into a women's bathroom in order to convince Ando he can really do such things. Fate, however, quickly intervenes once he sends himself to New York. There, he discovers Isaac Mendez's prophecies and learns he has a substantial role to play in saving the world.

STEPPING UP

Hiro ends up in New York's future. Followi[ng] clues in a *9th Wonders!* comic book, he discovers Isaac Mendez has been murdered and soon, the destruction of the city occurs. His power allows him to escape, realizing h[is] gift is a serious responsibility. He takes it u[pon] himself to prevent the future he witnessed.

FUTURE ROLE

Eventually, Hiro's power permits him to experience the seemingly impossible—he meets himself a few years into the future. His future self is somber and serious, focused almost exclusively on his mission. But the danger of the moment is not the only reason for his personality shift—in the future, he has lost his dear friend, Ando.

THE LEGACY

Hiro takes his quest to save the cheerleader so seriously he cannot be deterred—even by his stern and judgmental father. Seeking to repair Kensei's sword before going after Sylar, Hiro is confronted by his father. Kaito puts Hiro to the test—training him in the ancient combat arts. Kaito quickly realizes Hiro is no longer the silly boy he remembers—he is a man on a mission and worthy of the family legacy.

PROPHECY FULFILLED

Hiro finally achieves the goal he has long sought since seeing it prophesied in an Isaac Mendez drawing—he unhesitatingly runs his sword into Sylar's chest at Kirby Plaza. The act, he believes, prevents Sylar from exploding. Reality is a bit different, since Peter Petrelli is the actual exploding man. But Hiro's effort gives Peter the pause he needs to find a way to avoid detonating inside the city.

FORBIDDEN LOVE

Hiro finally shows his love for the swordsmith's daughter, Yaeko, in the year 1671. She falls in love with Hiro's heroic nature as he inspires her Takezo Kensei stories. But history says Yaeko is Kensei's lover. When Adam Monroe sees them kissing, he feels betrayed and turns from the heroic path.

ANDO MASAHASHI

Ando Masahashi may seem to be just a sidekick to his super-powered friend, Hiro Nakamura, but in truth, he's much more—he's proof that heroism is a state of mind, not a physical capability. At first, Ando has simple aspirations, typical of any young man, and he is skeptical about Hiro's abilities and quest. Still, even as that quest begins to dominate his life, Ando never wavers from supporting his friend and showing courage equal to Hiro's. His importance to Hiro is made clear in an alternate future timeline, where Future Hiro's life darkens following Ando's death.

- **Power: Supercharging Red Lightning (synthetically induced)**
- **Hometown: Tokyo, Japan**
- **Occupation: Computer programmer, Yamagato Industries**

Supercharging Red Lightning
1. Through the injection of a synthetic formula, Ando develops the power to emit red-coloured energy that supercharges the powers of other evolved humans struck by the beam.
2. The ability is only useful when combined with other evolved people, for example it enables a speedster to move so fast she can time travel.

ANDO SHOWS THAT COURAGE IS NOT DEPENDENT ON HAVING SPECIAL POWERS.

BEST FRIENDS
Ando is the constant spark of humor in Hiro's life, no matter what danger they face. Even while trying to talk Hiro out of some of his most dangerous stunts, Ando keeps his friend's disposition bright.

"YOU DON'T NEED SPECIAL POWERS TO BE A HERO."

FEARLESS
With Hiro unavailable, Ando decides he can't wait any longer to do something about Sylar, who is holed up in Isaac Mendez's loft. He purchases a sword and decides to confront the murderer by himself, despite the incredible danger. He bravely makes the attempt, but is overpowered and seconds from death when Hiro shows up and teleports him to safety.

ADAM MONROE

Adam Monroe discovers his immortality in Feudal Japan through an encounter with Hiro Nakamura. For 400 years, he travels the world, never aging, marrying repeatedly, and fighting countless battles. In 1977, he brings together the founders of the Company and concludes that genetically advanced people are superior. He then tries twice to cleanse humanity using the Shanti Virus, but is thwarted. Hiro imprisons him in a grave until Arthur Petrelli manipulates him into releasing him. Adam believes he cannot die, but his tale ends when Arthur takes his power, leaving him to crumble into dust.

- **Power: Rapid Cellular Regeneration**
- **Home: UK, but has lived all over the world**
- **Occupations: Dozens over the centuries, including Soldier, Mercenary, Sea captain, Samurai warrior, Plantation owner**

Rapid Cellular Regeneration
1. The ability to instantly regenerate cells to heal bodily injuries.
2. The body generates antibodies that are immune to all bacteria and viruses.
3. It can be hampered by foreign objects—if something is lodged in the brain, the subject can appear dead until it is removed.
4. It renders a subject essentially immortal.

> AT 400 YEARS OLD, ADAM IS ONE OF THE EARLIEST RECORDED GENETICALLY ADVANCED HUMAN BEINGS.

"I CUT MYSELF AND THE WOUND HEALS. OVER AND OVER AGAIN."

THE BEGINNING

Before learning of his special power, Adam is little more than a drunken con-man. Hiro changes his direction, however, cajoling him into using his power honorably. But when Adam feels betrayed by Hiro over a woman, he returns to a more selfish path.

10 WIVES

HELENE—1672—DIEDENSHAUSEN, GERMANY

MARIA—1747—MILAN, ITALY

FREDERICA—1782—VERSAILLES, FRANCE

YUMI (YAEKO'S GREAT-GRANDDAUGHTER)—1

ANGELICA—1787—NORTHWEST TERRITORY

MARIA—1864—ATLANTA, GA

DIANE—1901—MONTREAL, CANADA

LOUISA—1926—CHICAGO, IL

THERESA—1958—LOS ANGELES, CA

TRINA—1977

Some of Adam's wives leave him, fearful of his power, and a couple he abandons. One, Theresa, betrays him and pays for it with her life. Two, Angelica and Diane, are the loves of his long life. He is married to them for 62 years and 20 years, but they inevitably die, leaving him alone again.

THE LEGEND OF TAKEZO KENSEI

Historians postulate that the legendary Japanese warrior, Takezo Kensei, was probably a Samurai named Miyamoto Musashi who was defender of the innocent, foe of tyrants, dragon slayer, and swordsman without peer. But a time-traveling Hiro Nakamura, who has idolized Kensei since childhood, learns a different truth. Finding himself in Japan in 1671, he discovers that the "real" Kensei is a drunken, profiteering Englishman named Adam Monroe who later finds he possesses the genetic power of regeneration. Hiro tries to teach Adam to be the Kensei of legend, and even dons Kensei's armor in order to accomplish many of the famed deeds himself, inspiring Kensei's lover, Yaeko, to write stories that eventually take on the weight of historical fact.

TAKEZO KENSEI IS AN OLD JAPANESE LEGEND, BUT WHO ACTUALLY ACHIEVED HIS EXPLOITS IS LOST IN TIME.

HIRO AS HERO
When necessary, Hiro assumes the Kensei identity himself in order to maintain history's recording of the Kensei legend. Here, he uses his power to stop time in order to disarm twelve of White Beard's fighters in the famed Battle of Twelve Swords.

ANCIENT MESSAGE
Ando Masahashi finds scrolls written to him by his friend, Hiro, in the handle of Kensei's sword. He brings them to Tasuya Atsumi, curator of the Tokyo Museum of Cultural History, for analysis and restoration. On the scrolls, Hiro documents the story of his struggle to make Adam Monroe into history's Takezo Kensei, but some of the writing is faded or illegible. Atsumi helps Ando decipher them, only to be stymied as the story ends abruptly before its conclusion.

HIDDEN FORTRESS
Among Kensei's historic feats is his famed battle with 90 Angry Ronin, who guard the sacred Fire Scroll at the Hidden Fortress of his arch-foe, White Beard. Hiro helps Adam win the battle as legend indicates.

LEGENDARY LOVE
A woman named Yaeko finds nothing admirable in Takezo Kensei until Hiro shows up. To her, Hiro himself personifies the heroic ideal of Kensei, and she falls in love with him as a result. Their ill-fated relationship, however, drives a wedge between Hiro and Adam that reverberates for centuries.

ISAAC MENDEZ PREDICTS HIRO NAKAMURA'S DUEL WITH ADAM MONROE IN THE SIXTH OF HIS SERIES OF EIGHT PROPHETIC PAINTINGS.

"YOU ARE TAKEZO KENSEI! MY HERO! I MUST SAVE YOU!"

THE TWO FORMER FRIENDS BATTLE AFTER HIRO'S KISS WITH YAEKO LEADS ADAM TO SIDE WITH WHITE BEARD AGAINST HIRO.

ISAAC MENDEZ

Isaac Mendez prognosticates events long before they happen, and the impact of his predictive paintings reverberates to this day, especially since their meaning is frequently ambiguous. Isaac discovers his skill after painting the death of a stranger and other disturbing events, but his heroin addiction causes his girlfriend, Simone Deveaux, to doubt his gift. Despite success as a comic book author, Isaac feels he has wasted his life, but his ability to foretell—and help avert—disasters finally gives his life meaning and his death purpose.

- **Power: Precognition**
- **Hometown: New York City, NY**
- **Occupations: Artist; Comic book author and illustrator**

Precognition
1. The ability to perceive future events and paint or draw details of those happenings, while in deep concentration or a trance.
2. When in a clairvoyant state, he shows little or no awareness of the environment around him.

HEROIN ADDICT
At first, Isaac believes he can only use his power when high, so he thinks his habit is tied in with his destiny to save the world. Therefore, when Simone asks him to choose between her and heroin, he chooses the drug. With help from Eden McCain while in the Company's custody, he finally manages to kick his habit and learns how to use his ability without drugs.

HIS VALUABLE ABILITY TO "PAINT THE FUTURE" PLACES ISAAC IN THE MIDDLE OF HUMANITY'S STRUGGLE.

"WHAT GOOD IS PAINTING THE FUTURE, IF NO ONE WILL DO ANYTHING TO CHANGE IT?"

TRANCE
When painting the future, Isaac enters a deep precognitive trance that glazes his eyes and takes over his entire consciousness—he is able to focus only on the images traveling from his mind to the canvas.

THE IMPORTANCE OF HIS ABILITY BECOMES CLEAR TO ISAAC WHEN HE SEES A MEDIA PHOTOGRAPH OF A TERRORIST BOMBING IN ISRAEL THAT EXACTLY MATCHES ONE OF HIS PAINTINGS.

ISAAC'S PAINTINGS CAN BE EASILY MISREAD. THIS IMAGE DOES NOT FORETELL A SUICIDE, AS IT MAY APPEAR. RATHER, IT REVEALS THE EXISTENCE OF ANOTHER EVOLVED ATTRIBUTE—FLIGHT—AND IT CONVINCES PETER PETRELLI HE HAS THAT ABILITY.

TROUBLED RELATIONSHIP

Despite his love for Simone, Isaac can't defeat his demons and the pressures on him long enough to save their relationship. His heroin habit, her incredulity about his ability and need to save the world, and finally Peter Petrelli come between them. Convinced that Peter is a threat, Isaac attempts to shoot him, but tragically kills Simone instead.

COMIC CLUES

Isaac Mendez's work becomes a tool in the struggle to save the world. His predictive drawings in his comic *9th Wonders!* help guide Hiro Nakamura on his journey.

"I FINALLY KNOW MY PART IN THIS. TO DIE, LIKE THIS. I FINALLY GET TO BE A HERO."

PROPHECY OF DEATH

After Simone dies, Isaac's power brings the realization that his end is also near when he paints the gruesome vision of his own death at Sylar's hands. Ironically, the image brings relief—it lets him focus on painting visions of Sylar's defeat to aid Hiro. Thus, when his final encounter with Sylar comes, Isaac accepts death with grace, feeling as though he is a hero at last.

AS WELL AS BEING AMBIGUOUS, THE SIGNIFICANCE OF ISAAC'S PAINTINGS IS FREQUENTLY NOT CLEAR. HERE, THE PAINTING OF SIMONE GIVES NO CLUE THAT SHE IS JUST MOMENTS AWAY FROM AN UNTIMELY DEATH.

FROM THE EXPLODING MAN TO A LETHAL VIRUS OUTBREAK, ISAAC'S PAINTINGS REVEAL DEVASTATING FUTURE EVENTS. ISAAC CANNOT PREVENT THEM ON HIS OWN, BUT HIS IMAGES FOREWARN OTHERS WHO DO HAVE THE POWER TO HELP.

NATHAN PETRELLI

Nathan Petrelli's leadership abilities and his family lineage make him a central player in the evolutionary conflict he inadvertently joins at birth, thanks to his father's machinations. When he saves New York, Nathan fights against letting individuals or organizations decide humanity's fate. But after being shot, and later witnessing the cruelty of a super-powered Haitian despot, he reverses course and pursues that objective himself. Facing opposition, Nathan initiates a draconian plan to eliminate evolved people who could pose a threat, including even his own brother, Peter.

- Power: Self-propelled Flight (synthetically induced)
- Hometown: Hyde Park, NY
- Occupations: US Navy Officer; New York District Attorney; US Congressman; US Senator representing New York

Self-propelled Flight
1. The ability to fly, self-propelled, at high altitudes and high speeds over long distances, possibly at near supersonic speeds.
2. The power was developed in Nathan synthetically by Company scientists soon after his birth.
3. at least to a degree, the ability appears to protect him from temperature extremes and atmospheric pressure.

"WHEN THE TIME COMES, VOTE PETRELLI."

FIRST FLIGHT
Nathan's plans to expose his father's dealings with Daniel Linderman lead to great trauma. To silence him, hired thugs cause his car to crash, leaving his wife, Heidi, paralyzed. But Nathan is unhurt as the event causes his power of flight to manifest for the first time.

HEALING MANIPULATION
Linderman uses his healing power to cure Heidi's paralysis. It's supposedly a gift, but in reality, it's part of his ongoing manipulation of Nathan—whom he is grooming to play a central role in the future.

REPEATED ENCOUNTERS WITH HIRO NAKAMURA INFLUENCE NATHAN PETRELLI TO CONSIDER THE POSSIBILITY THAT THE DESTRUCTION OF NEW YORK IS NOT INEVITABLE, AND THAT HE HAS A RESPONSIBILITY TO DO THE RIGHT THING.

NATHAN WANTS TO PROTECT HUMANITY, BUT HE IS CAPABLE OF CHOOSING TOTALITARIAN AND MORALLY DUBIOUS SOLUTIONS.

GIVEN LINDERMAN'S BALLOT FIXING, IT'S NOT CLEAR HOW NATHAN'S POLITICAL CAREER MIGHT HAVE ADVANCED ON ITS OWN MERITS.

Petrelli Throws His Hat into Congressional Ring

"EVERYONE'S ENTITLED TO THEIR SECRETS."

PURSUIT OF POWER

For high-flying, ambitious Nathan, politics is an obvious choice, and his military service, family heritage, and success as District Attorney allow him to pursue that dream. He wins a Congressional seat from New York's 14th District, albeit after Linderman rigs the vote. After events at Kirby Plaza, badly injured, he resigns. Later, the Governor of New York appoints him to an open US Senate seat.

COMING TOGETHER

After he prevents Tracy Strauss from committing suicide, Nathan grows close to her. He helps her come to grips with her newly discovered power, and they soon enter into a highly consequential relationship. Tracy takes steps to get Nathan appointed to the US Senate, and later, influences him into joining his father's dangerous organization, the Pinehearst Company.

FATEFUL MOMENT

Nathan calls a press conference to announce the existence of evolved humans, but he's shot in the chest before he reveals it. The assailant: his own brother, from the future, trying to alter a tragic timeline.

DANIEL LINDERMAN URGES NATHAN TO ACCEPT HIS PLAN TO DESTROY NEW YORK AND HELP NATHAN ASCEND TO GREAT POWER—EVEN, AT ONE POINT, SHOWING HIM AN ISAAC MENDEZ PAINTING AT OF NATHAN AS PRESIDENT.

CHOOSING HIS OWN DESTINY, A RAPIDLY WEAKENING NATHAN FLIES HIS BROTHER PETER HIGH ABOVE NEW YORK CITY AS HE GETS READY TO DETONATE, SAVING NEW YORK FROM DESTRUCTION.

PETER PETRELLI

Underestimated by almost everyone, Peter Petrelli is not the most likely person to become a globally consequential figure. However, once he learns to control his powers, he becomes incredibly potent, but with heavy burdens to shoulder. Grappling with these splits him from his brother and father, destroys two women he loves, involves him with a violent killer, absorbs him twice in events that almost result in horrific destruction, and cause him to glimpse his future murder. Yet, passionate and principled, he refuses to accept the inevitably of anything and perseveres, laboring tirelessly to save the world.

- **Power: Empathic Mimicry, leading to many other abilities**
- **Hometown: New York City, NY**
- **Occupations: Former student; Former hospice nurse**

Empathic Mimicry
1. The ability to copy and permanently maintain the powers of other evolved humans.
2. Unlike his father, Peter takes power without removing it from its original
3. With training, he learns to keep the power active after leaving its donor's vicinity and to use multiple powers at the same time.
4. Peter's first acquired skill is believed to be is his mother's precognitive drea

"I'VE BEEN TRYING TO SAVE THE WORLD ONE PERSON AT A TIME. BUT I'M MEANT FOR SOMETHING BIGGER. SOMETHING IMPORTANT. I KNOW IT NOW."

UNLIKELY MENTOR
Tormented by possessing power he can't control, Peter one day sees a man that no one else can—he's known as Claude Rains, and he's invisible. A disenchanted Company operative in hiding, Claude reluctantly mentors Peter in learning how to manage his abilities.

BROTHERS
Peter and his brother Nathan clearly love each other, but from the moment they discover their abilities, they repeatedly diverge ideologically on what to do about the threats facing the world. In time, a traumatic split opens between the two.

PETER USES HIS INVISIBILITY TO AVOID SYLAR DURING THEIR FIRST ENCOUNTER, BUT THE MURDERER SHOWERS THE ROOM WITH GLASS AND GRIEVOUSLY WOUNDS HIM.

FATE DRAWS PETER INTO CIRCULAR BATTLES. SOMETIMES HE CAUSES EVENTS HE SEEKS TO PREVENT, OR BECOMES ENTANGLED IN UNANTICIPATED, DISASTROUS OUTCOMES.

IN IRELAND, CAITLIN WATCHES AS PETER, IN A PRECOGNITIVE TRANCE, PAINTS A SCENE IN MONTREAL—A CLUE TO WHAT THEY SHOULD DO NEXT.

"DON'T YOU GET IT? EVERYTHING'S CONNECTED. WE'RE ALL CONNECTED."

FUTURE PETER

A future timeline's Peter Petrelli is hard-edged, scarred, and angry. He has lived through a violent crackdown against people with enhanced abilities. He even sees himself hunted and attacked by someone he loves very much. All this convinces him to travel through time to violently attack his own brother—somehow believing that doing so will correct the timeline.

PROPHETIC EMBRACE

Among the key events predicted in paintings created by the African precog, Usutu, is the moment in which Peter Petrelli succumbs to an embrace from his father, and as a result, loses his powers. Usutu paints the event shortly before it happens inside the Pinehearst Building and shows it to Hiro Nakamura, along with another painting illustrating the villains assembled at Pinehearst.

PETER AMAZES EVEN HIMSELF WHEN HE MASTERS HIS TELEKINETIC POWER TO THE DEGREE WHERE HE CAN ACTUALLY STOP BULLETS IN MID-AIR BEFORE THEY

WHEN SURPRISED BY ADAM MONROE IN MONTREAL, PETER LASHES OUT BY GENERATING A BURST OF ELECTRICITY. MONROE IS UNHARMED

PRECOGNITIVE DREAMING from his mother, Angela Petrelli

INDUCED RADIOACTIVITY—emitting radioactive energy—from Ted Sprague

PETER'S POWERS

Peter Petrelli is possibly the most powerful human being in history. His manifest skill is called empathic mimicry, but he took a long time to realize he possessed it, and even longer to comprehend the nature of the power and how to control it, both physically and emotionally. Here is a sampling of the many capabilities that Peter has mimicked, although it's possible he has other powers—perhaps some that he doesn't even realize he has.

SPACE/TIME MANIPULATION acquired from Hiro Nakamura

POWER DAMPENING—blocking powers of others—acquired from the Haitian

TELEPATHY acquired from Matt Parkman

"I TOOK HIS POWER. I CAN'T CONTROL IT."

SUPERHUMAN STRENGTH acquired from Niki Sanders

PRECOGNITION—the ability to paint the future—from Isaac Mendez

RAPID CELLULAR REGENERATION from Claire Bennet

INVISIBILITY from the man called Claude Rains

PHASING—passing through people and objects, from D.L. Hawkins

ELECTRICAL MANIPULATION from Elle Bishop

FLIGHT from his brother, Nathan Petrelli

VOCAL PERSUASION from Eden McCain

FREEZING acquired from Tracy Strauss

ENHANCED SENSES acquired from Mohinder Suresh

PYROKINESIS—combustable flame manipulation—from the criminal known as Flint

INTUITIVE APTITUDE—instant comprehension of how things work—from Sylar

CLAIRE BENNET

Claire Bennet spent the first sixteen years of her life unaware of the latent abilities within her. When they finally manifest, the carefree teenager quickly learns that with them comes heartbreak. A deranged killer targets her, the Company obsesses over her, and, as the host of a mysterious Catalyst, she becomes the key to creating a dangerous Formula. Along the way, Claire's adoptive father deceives her, and she loses homes, friends, and her innocence. Ultimately, a new Claire emerges—stronger and more heroic, but potentially more fearsome.

- **Power: Rapid Cellular Regeneration**
- **Hometown: Odessa, TX; Costa Verde, CA; New York City, NY**
- **Occupation: High school student**

Rapid Cellular Regeneration

1. The ability to regenerate cells to heal bodily injuries.
2. She can generate antibodies giving immunity to all bacteria and viruses.
3. The power can be hampered by foreign objects—if something is lodged in the brain, the subject can appear dead until it is removed.
4. It renders a subject essentially immortal.

ADOPTED FAMILY

Sandra, Lyle, and Noah Bennet are the only family Claire knows, and they love her deeply. But she has a murky past to resolve. The need to understand her power and where she comes from drives her to explore her origins, despite her adoptive father's efforts to protect her from the truth.

> "I'VE BUSTED EVERY BONE IN MY BODY, STABBED MYSELF IN THE CHEST, SHOVED A TWO-FOOT STEEL ROD THROUGH MY NECK AND THERE'S NOT A SCRATCH ON ME."

REAL MOM

Claire's investigation of her past leads to her biological mother, Meredith Gordon, a former Company agent with the power of pyrokinesis. She learns she is the product of a brief affair between Meredith and Nathan Petrelli (inset). Meredith believed her daughter dead after a Company operation went wrong when Claire was an infant. Only the Company knew she was alive, and they placed her in the Bennet household.

MANY CALL CLAIRE BENNET "THE CHEERLEADER," AND SHE INITIALLY PREFERS THE NORMALCY OF THAT ROLE. IN THE END, THOUGH, SHE'S DESTINED FOR GREATER THINGS.

CLAIRE IS A REPEATED IMAGE IN ISAAC MENDEZ'S WORK—AS A MYSTERIOUS, FEARFUL CHEERLEADER, PURSUED BY A MENACING FIGURE. THE PAINTINGS HELP OTHER HEROES REALIZE THEY MUST SAVE HER TO SAVE THE WORLD.

STARTING OVER IN COSTA VERDE, CLAIRE GETS HER WISH TO BECOME A CHEERLEADER AND PURSUE A "NORMAL" EXISTENCE. BUT WHEN SHE MEETS ANOTHER SUPER-POWERED PERSON, SHE REALIZES THAT AN ORDINARY LIFE IS BEYOND HER GRASP.

THE BEGINNING

Company chief Kaito Nakamura orders Noah Bennet to raise baby Claire and monitor her for signs of a genetic manifestation. Noah initially balks, but eventually, Claire becomes his life.

"I'VE DIED BEFORE. IT'S NO BIG DEAL."

MIRACLE POWER

Claire watches unconcerned as her burned, bleeding hands heal in a matter of seconds after a cooking accident. It is an increasingly typical scene in her unusual life.

GENETIC SECRETS

Claire feels physical pain for one of the last times in her life as Sylar opens her skull in search of her power. Unlike his past victims, however, Claire can't die. Thus, she's conscious as Sylar probes her brain and realizes there is something "different" about her genetic makeup. When he's done, Claire can no longer feel pain.

IN COSTA VERDE CLAIRE MEETS A BOY NAMED WEST, WHO HAS A SPECIAL ABILITY OF HIS OWN—FLYING. IF NOT NORMALCY, CLAIRE HOPES THAT SHE MIGHT HAVE FOUND LOVE, AND SOMEONE WHO UNDERSTANDS HER.

IN THE FUTURE, PEOPLE WITH POWERS MUST HIDE FROM THE GOVERNMENT, SO CLAIRE TRANSFORMS INTO A WAITRESS NAMED SANDRA AT THE BURNT TOAST DINER. HOWEVER, EVEN THERE, SHE IS NOT SAFE.

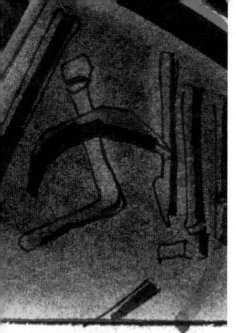

GIRL on the AUTOPSY TABLE

The mystery cheerleader who keeps appearing in Isaac Mendez's prophetic paintings is Claire Bennet. Here, Isaac foresees her death and autopsy—but not her resurrection. When a date with popular quarterback Brody Mitchum turns into an attempted rape, Claire's head is impaled on a tree branch and she ends up at the mortuary. But once the object is removed, Claire's indestructible body revives and she slips away. When it becomes clear that Brody has attacked others—and will continue to—Claire actively uses her power to punish him for what he did. She drives his car, with him in it, into a wall at high speed. In the hospital, her revengeful father, Noah Bennet, with help from the Haitian, wipes Brody's entire memory so he doesn't even know what his name is.

NIKI SANDERS

Niki Sanders was not supposed to be super-powered—she and her triplet sisters Tracy and Barbara were genetically manipulated before birth by Company scientist, Dr. Zimmerman. Over time Niki struggles with alcoholism, money issues, a turbulent marriage, and a young son. Childhood abuse leads to a personality disorder in the form of an alter-ego named Jessica, who lands her in trouble with gangsters, the law, and her family. Eventually, she purges her alter-ego, but later develops a new one, which results in tragedy.

- **Power: Superhuman Strength (synthetically induced before birth)**
- **Hometown: Beverly Hills, CA; relocates to Las Vegas, NV**
- **Occupations: Internet stripper; Casino worker; Car salesman; Fugitive from justice; Company operative**

Superhuman Strength
1. The ability to perform feats of incredible brute force, including ripping people literally apart, knocking down doors and walls, ripping open a safe with her bare hands, and breaking out of handcuffs.
2. She appears to have a heightened sense of speed, coordination, physical durability, and aggression when in action.

NIKI APPEARS TOO WEAK TO SUPPRESS HER ALTER-EGO'S PERSONALITY, BUT IN THE END, HER INNER STRENGTH PREVAILS.

"I WAKE UP AND THINGS AREN'T... LIKE THEY WERE."

SPLIT PERSONALITY
Niki's personality disorder result in an intense struggle between th Niki and Jessica personalities for control of her body and highly dangerous skill. The disorder permits whichever personality is dominant to communicate with the other personality reflected in mirrors. Initially, Jessica's force of will allows only her, and not Niki, to utilize her body's incredible power—something she does repeatedly, with deadly efficiency.

JESSICA SANDERS DIED IN 1987 AT THE AGE OF 11 AT THE HANDS OF HER ABUSIVE FATHER, HAL. THE TRAUMA OF THE EVENT CAUSES NIKI'S PSYCHOLOGICAL DISORDER TO EMERGE, WITH JESSICA AT THE CENTER OF IT.

NIKI'S HUSBAND, D.L., STEADFASTLY BELIEVES IN HER, EVEN AS HER ILLNESS ESSENTIALLY DESTROYS HIS LIFE. TORN BETWEEN PROTECTING MICAH FROM JESSICA AND BEING WITH NIKI, HE CONTINUALLY WORKS TO HELP HER REGAIN CONTROL.

PRIDE AND JOY
The most important force in Niki's drive to get healthy is her son, Micah. Protecting him is her prime mission, but her situation inadvertently keeps putting him in danger.

DEADLY EMERGENCE
Desperate for money, Niki begins a small business stripping on the Internet. Her alter-ego, Jessica, on the other hand, pulls off a major heist to get cash—ripping off mafia boss Daniel Linderman himself. This causes his men to come hard after Niki. They finally corner her, rough her up, and force her to strip. This proves to be their undoing, however, since their actions trigger a transformation into the Jessica personality. None of Linderman's men survive their encounter with

UNSTABLE
Unable to control Jessica, Niki turns herself in to the authorities. Jessica soon emerges and attacks a psychiatrist, but the manipulative Linderman arranges her release because he needs her to play a bigger role in his plans.

"I CAN'T BE TRUSTED."

NIKI DOESN'T HESITATE TO RUSH INTO A BURNING BUILDING TO SAVE HER NIECE, MONICA DAWSON. FINALLY FREE OF HER PSYCHOLOGICAL DEMONS, NIKI HEROICALLY GIVES HER LIFE IN THIS ONE SELFLESS ACT.

NIKI'S SON, MICAH, AND NIECE, MONICA, WATCH IN HORROR AS THE BUILDING WHERE MONICA HAD BEEN HELD PRISONER EXPLODES IN A GIGANTIC FIREBALL BEFORE NIKI CAN GET OUT.

JESSICA'S EXPLOITS

There are many unexplained questions about Niki Sanders' alter-ego, known as Jessica—an ultra-aggressive, super-strong, adult version of Niki's dead young sister. What is clear, however, is that when Jessica emerges, she's prone to acts of extreme violence. Before Jessica disappears from Niki's life, she wreaks a massive path of havoc. Along the way, she robs Linderman, pinning the theft on Niki's husband, D.L.; shoots D.L.; kills Linderman's thugs; works as an assassin for Linderman, shooting two Federal agents in the process; assaults Matt Parkman; sexually blackmails Nathan Petrelli; beats the hell out of her father, Hal; and attacks the psychotherapist who is trying to help her.

"YOU HAVE TO ADMIT, NIKI. I DO A BETTER YOU THAN YOU."

DANGEROUS LIAISON

Fugitive D.L. Hawkins returns home from jail initially unaware of the danger posed by Jessica. He doesn't realize she's the reason he's wanted for murder and theft. She steals $2 million from Daniel Linderman, working with D.L.'s crew, but then slaughters them when they turn on her. The authorities blame D.L., and Jessica appears perfectly willing to sacrifice him to preserve what she considers "her" family.

TRAPPED

Niki watches helplessly from "the other side" while her alter-ego, Jessica, takes over her life. For a long time, Niki remained in control, but was tormented by the threatening Jessica, who communicated with her through any reflective surface. Later, though, when her husband, D.L., leaves with their son, Micah, Jessica asserts control and goes after D.L., while Niki remains trapped behind the mirror.

BLACKMAIL

The internal conflict between Niki and Jessica bubbles over when a desperate Niki agrees to seduce Nathan Petrelli so that Linderman will forgive her debt. Niki can't go through with it, but Jessica surfaces and pulls off the seduction… on videotape. Later, Linderman hires Jessica to assassinate Nathan, but this time, Niki's will wins out, and Nathan is spared.

MORAL DILEMMA

Jessica claims that her terrifying acts are in Niki's best interests, even though they wreak havoc on her already complicated life. Niki watches in horror as Jessica does what she thinks best. However, when Linderman offers Jessica $20 million to kill D.L., she finally relents from her rampage of violence and refuses, recognizing how much Niki loves him.

MICAH SANDERS

Child prodigy Micah Sanders is the consequence of Daniel Linderman's manipulation of his parents—Niki Sanders and D.L. Hawkins. Wise beyond his years, Micah sometimes seems to be the only level-headed one in his chaotic family. Despite their love for him, his parents struggle to give him a stable and secure life. However, Micah's maturity and special skill help him cope with the upheaval and danger—even surviving kidnapping and manipulation by Linderman. Still, nothing can prepare him for the untimely deaths of both his parents.

- **Power: Technopathy**
- **Hometown: Las Vegas, NV; relocates to New Orleans, LA**
- **Status: Grade school student**

Technopathy
1. The ability to control electronic devices and machinery through mental manipulation, using a slight touch and deep concentration.
2. He is capable of controlling devices connected through computer networks by touching a single device on that network, or even through physical contact with a telephone dialed into that network.

DESPITE HIS YOUTH, MICAH HAS A MORE SOPHISTICATED ATTITUDE TOWARDS HIS POWERS THAN MOST.

MOTHER

Micah's mother, Niki Sanders, is simultaneously Micah's closest confidante and, due to her psychological illness, the source of much of his pain. Their bond is extra close because, with D.L. away, they spent so much time in each other's company.

FATHER

Micah never stops believing in his father, D.L. Hawkins, even when he is framed on murder and theft charges. When Niki is in jail, father and son struggle at first to cope on their own, but they soon learn to work together and Micah confides in D.L. about his special skill.

SHORTLY AFTER HIS MOTHER'S DEATH, MICAH MEETS TRACY STRAUSS—HIS MOM'S IDENTICAL SISTER. MICAH INTUITIVELY COMPREHENDS SHE IS A RELATIVE, BUT NOT HIS MOTHER.

GREAT AUNT

Nana Dawson is Micah's great aunt, and the glue that holds her family together after the tragedy of Hurricane Katrina. She doesn't hesitate in accepting Micah into her home after D.L.'s death, when Niki reluctantly leaves him behind to seek help from the Company for her personality disorder.

KINDRED SPIRIT

Micah instantly bonds with his cousin, Monica Dawson, when he goes to live in New Orleans. He recognizes her struggle to understand her unique skill, and helps her learn to accept it. When Micah loses a priceless treasure, she risks her life to retrieve it and when she runs into more trouble than she bargained for, Micah tries to come to her rescue.

"YOU KNOW HOW YOU AND MOM HAVE A SECRET? WELL I HAVE A SECRET TOO."

DESPERATE MEASURES

Living with his father after his mother turns herself in to police, Micah becomes desperate to help ease the family's financial crisis. He reluctantly decides to use his power to get a large amount of cash out of an ATM machine.

MICAH'S POWER ALLOWS HIM TO USE A BROKEN PAY PHONE, SUMMON AN ELEVATOR, TRIGGER AN ATM MACHINE, RIG VOTING MACHINES, AND MUCH MORE.

MICAH GAINS SOME RESPECT FROM HIS COUSIN, DAMON, WHEN HE COMMANDS THE FAMILY'S CABLE BOX TO SHOW A PAY-PER -VIEW WRESTLING MATCH.

D.L. HAWKINS

The son of an evolved woman, Paulette Hawkins, who died mysteriously in a Company operation, Daniel Lawrence or "D.L." Hawkins is a loyal family man. Although his wife Niki's alter ego, Jessica, frames him as a thief and murderer and forces him into a deadly confrontation with Linderman, D.L. risks everything to protect Niki and their son, Micah. Despite gunshot wounds, he kills Linderman, rescues Micah, and finds stability in a job as a firefighter. Sadly, Niki's personality disorder returns, and D.L.'s refusal to abandon her brings about his tragic death.

- **Power: Phasing**
- **Hometown: Las Vegas, NV**
- **Occupations: Construction worker; briefly involved with a criminal gang; Firefighter**

Phasing
1. The ability to pass, or phase, any part of his body through any type of solid matter by instantly rendering his molecular composition intangible.
2. He can also phase other people through solid matter as long as they are in physical contact with him.

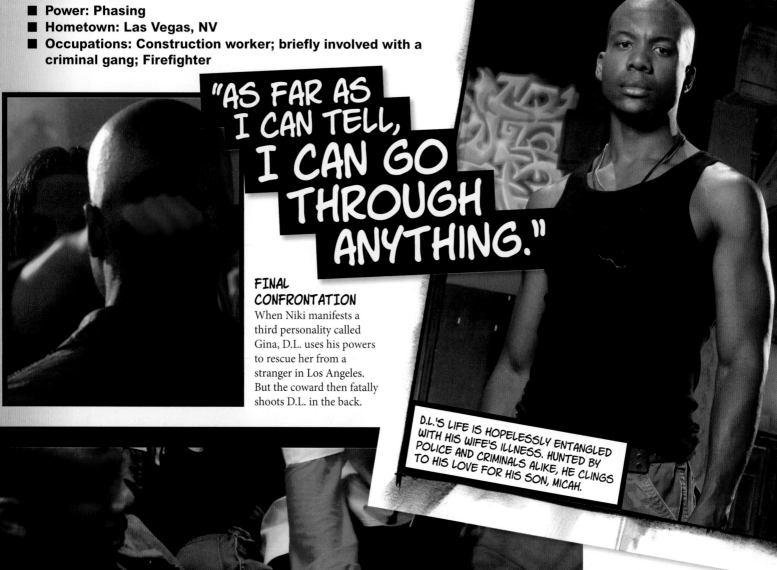

"AS FAR AS I CAN TELL, I CAN GO THROUGH ANYTHING."

FINAL CONFRONTATION
When Niki manifests a third personality called Gina, D.L. uses his powers to rescue her from a stranger in Los Angeles. But the coward then fatally shoots D.L. in the back.

D.L.'S LIFE IS HOPELESSLY ENTANGLED WITH HIS WIFE'S ILLNESS. HUNTED BY POLICE AND CRIMINALS ALIKE, HE CLINGS TO HIS LOVE FOR HIS SON, MICAH.

CLOSE CALL
A near holocaust at Kirby Plaza is averted, but D.L.'s fate remains in the balance. He's in danger of bleeding to death after intentionally taking a bullet from Linderman's gun that was meant for his wife, Niki. Doctors save his life, giving him a few more precious months with his family, but he won't be so fortunate next time.

RARE ROSE

Monica's copycat ability first manifests when she absent-mindedly carves this perfect rose out of a tomato after seeing it done on television. She later emulates a wrestling move and Micah's piano playing skill before fully comprehending the nature of her talent.

TROUBLED ALL HER LIFE BY INJUSTICE AND UNFAIRNESS, MONICA DAWSON YEARNS TO MAKE A DIFFERENCE.

ST. JOAN

Micah's rare *9th Wonders!* comic book features a character with Monica's skills named St. Joan. When Micah's backpack containing the comic and his Dad's medal is stolen, she adopts St. Joan's approach and methods in order to retrieve it.

"I'M SUPPOSED TO BE SOMEBODY."

MONICA DAWSON

Since Hurricane Katrina devastated her family and hometown, Monica Dawson has yearned to educate herself and do something substantial with her life. It isn't until her cousin, Micah Sanders, comes to live with her that she manifests her unique ability and learns how special she really is. She quickly comes to the attention of the Company, and the organization helps her understand her power. As a result, Monica has the confidence to challenge thugs who rip off Micah. However, this leads to disaster as Monica is captured, and Niki Sanders perishes during the rescue attempt.

- **Power: Adoptive Muscle Memory**
- **Hometown: New Orleans, LA**
- **Occupation: Waitress in a fast food restaurant**

Adoptive Muscle Memory
1. The ability to flawlessly and instantly replicate any physical movement she sees, as long as it is within her body's physical capabilities.
2. The skill works automatically, whether in person, or viewed from afar on a television or computer screen, even if she is not concentrating on the movement.

MATT PARKMAN

Abandoned by his father, held back by dyslexia, and cheated on by his wife, Matt develops a fragile ego and a deep sense of failure. When his ability manifests, it initially makes a confused Matt flounder more as it exacerbates his problems while he struggles to understand his evolution—culminating in the loss of his marriage and job. Later mastering his ability and fears, Matt overcomes these setbacks and several attempts on his life and fulfills his heroic potential, leading to a shot at happiness alongside Daphne Millbrook.

- Power: Telepathy, later develops Advanced Telepathy
- Hometown: Los Angeles, CA; relocates to New York City, NY
- Occupations: LAPD Police officer; Private security; NYPD Detective

Telepathy
1. The ability to read minds, and communicate thoughts and feelings to others without using speech, writing, or touch.
2. Through practice, Matt develops advanced telepathy—the ability to control thoughts of others, manipulating them into doing things (persuasion) or changing their perception of reality (illusion)—even trapping them in illusions.

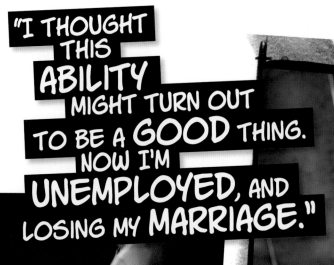

"I THOUGHT THIS ABILITY MIGHT TURN OUT TO BE A GOOD THING. NOW I'M UNEMPLOYED, AND LOSING MY MARRIAGE."

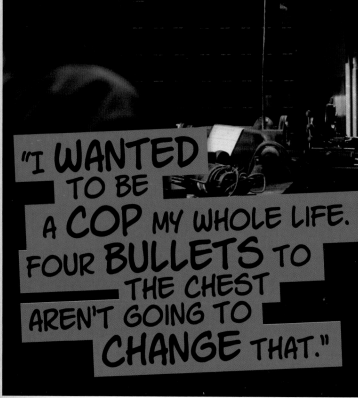

"I WANTED TO BE A COP MY WHOLE LIFE. FOUR BULLETS TO THE CHEST AREN'T GOING TO CHANGE THAT."

CRIME FIGHTER
Even after his power emerges, Parkman considers himself a cop first. When he encounters super-powered villains, they try to kill him, and sometimes to recruit him, but Matt's sense of justice never wavers. He goes after Sylar and the Company, tracks the killer of Kaito Nakamura and former Company members, then sets his course to stopping Arthur Petrelli and Pinehearst.

DRAFTED INTO THE SYLAR INVESTIGATION, MATT TEMPORARILY WORKS WITH FBI AGENT AUDREY HANSON, WHO IS OPEN-MINDED ABOUT HIS CRAZY ABILITY IF IT HELPS HER CATCH THE MURDERER.

MATT'S ABILITY ENABLES HIM TO PASS MESSAGES TO TED SPRAGUE FROM HIS DYING WIFE, EVEN THOUGH SHE IS IN A COMA, WHICH LETS THE COUPLE SAY GOODBYE.

PROTECTOR

While securing a Sylar murder scene, Matt Parkman's mind hears thoughts of a scared child. He follows the voice and locates Molly Walker. Initially, this puts Matt under suspicion, and later leads to the FBI bringing him into their hunt for Sylar. But it also has another consequence—it begins a deep and unbreakable familial bond with the girl. Matt becomes her hero, repeatedly rescues her, and eventually becomes her guardian.

FAILED MARRIAGE

Matt's ability brings him closer to his estranged wife, Janice, as he can now satisfy her desires, especially once he learns she's pregnant. However, it also lets him discover her infidelity with a senior colleague, Tom McHenry. When Matt realizes her baby is not his, he leaves, seeking a new life in New York.

SPIRIT WALK

Banished to a remote corner of Africa by the future version of Peter Petrelli, Matt encounters the precog Usutu. The African speaks in cryptic messages, but he guides Matt on a Spirit Walk, helping him understand that his destiny involves fighting to save the world, while finding love with the speedster Daphne Millbrook.

A MIND READER AT FIRST, MATT'S ENCOUNTER WITH HIS FATHER, SPIRIT WALK, AND TRAINING TEACH HIM HE'S FAR MORE POWERFUL—HE CAN CONTROL PEOPLE'S THOUGHTS.

MIND CONTROL GIVES MATT A POWERFUL INTERROGATION TOOL. NOT ONLY DOES HE KNOW WHETHER A SUSPECT IS LYING—HE CAN FORCE THEM TO REVEAL SECRETS, AS HE DOES WITH ANGELA PETRELLI.

TED SPRAGUE

Theodore Sprague epitomizes what can happen when awesome power suddenly takes hold in an unsuspecting individual. Sprague's ability to emit a destructive radioactive force manifests itself before he realizes it, causing him to leak radiation and kill the person he loves most—his wife Karen—with a deadly cancer. Enraged, confused, and grief-stricken, he hungers for someone to blame, eventually setting his sights on Noah Bennet and the Company. He meets others with special abilities, and begins a quest to take down the Company before a fatal encounter with the murderous Sylar.

- **Power: Induced Radioactivity**
- **Hometown: Los Angeles, CA**
- **Occupation: Medical equipment salesman**

Induced Radioactivity
1. The ability to cause spontaneous disintegration of microsco[pic] radionuclides, resulting in the emission of ionizing radiation a[t] levels up to, and possibly exceeding 2,000 curies.
2. The potential to spontaneously trigger nuclear-size explosio[ns] highly agitated.

"I'VE KILLED PEOPLE WITH MY POWER. I DIDN'T MEAN TO, BUT IT HAPPENED."

GOING NUCLEAR

Traumatized and confused, a revenge-seeking Ted can no longer control the explosive force raging within him. Consumed with lashing out at the Company, he is overcome with emotion and sets the Bennet's home ablaze. Only the power and bravery of Claire Bennet prevents worse tragedy, as she runs through fire to tranquilize Sprague.

SPRAGUE'S POWER MAKES HIM A WIDOWER, A MURDERER, A TERRORIST SUSPECT HUNTED BY THE FBI, AND A VICTIM OF SYLAR.

SPRAGUE'S END

In the waning moments of his life, a shackled Ted Sprague hangs helplessly in a crashed police van, while Sylar closes in thirsting for his power. Sylar, having manipulated Sprague's arrest in New York, strikes as Sprague is being transported t[o] a special holding facility designed to contain his abilit[y.]

HANA GITELMAN

Tragedy, duty, sacrifice, and her ability to act as a human electronic transmitter all led to Hana Gitelman's hard life as a soldier. Granddaughter of a Nazi-fighting partisan and daughter of one of Israel's first female fighter pilots, she saw them both killed by terrorists and her desire for revenge opens her to Noah Bennet's overtures. Betrayed by the Company, she later sacrifices herself—twice—to bring it down. Her first attack takes out a tracking satellite, but costs her physical body. However, she is able to survive bodiless in cyberspace. This digital essence dies in her cyber-strike at the Company's central hard drive.

- **Power: Cyberpathy—the ability to manipulate digital data**
- **Hometown: Jerusalem, Israel**
- **Occupations: Soldier, the Israeli Defense Forces; Mossad agent**

"SATELLITE SIGNALS. WI-FI. RADIO WAVES. A COMPUTER DOWNLOADS THEM. SO CAN I."

HANA GITELMAN CAN MANAGE, SORT, AND READ TRILLIONS OF TERABYTES OF DIGITAL DATA AS IT STREAMS THROUGH HER CEREBRAL CORTEX.

MISSION PLANNING

Hana Gitelman recruits others with grudges against the Company—Matt Parkman and Ted Sprague. She sets them off in pursuit of Noah Bennet, and departs on her own mission, to hunt the Company's founders.

SUPERMAN MOMENT

West Rosen sweeps Claire Bennet into his arms and soars with her high above Costa Verde, California, enjoying their affection and special bond. He uses his power to wow her with a "first date" on top of the Hollywood sign, where the pair finally learn to overcome their mutual fears and secrets and trust each other. Their joy, sadly, will be short lived as Claire never manages to have a "normal" life for long.

WEST ROSEN

West Rosen revels in his unusual ability and considers himself above the usual high-school trivia. He reveals his secret to Claire when she transfers to Costa Verde High School. In fact, he has a longer history with Claire than he realizes—they met when he was "bagged and tagged" as a child by Noah Bennet, but the Haitian wiped their memories. Despite their friendship—all the stronger for the fact they can truly be themselves around each other—West treasures his secret life above all else. So, when Claire considers going public, he flies out of her life.

- **Power: Self-propelled Flight**
- **Hometown: St. Louis, MO; relocates to Costa Verde, CA**

UNLIKE MANY PEOPLE WITH EXTRAORDINARY ABILITIES, WEST CONSIDERS BEING

REVENGE

Matt Parkman is paired with Ted Sprague by Hana Gitelman to seek answers about the Company. When they invade the Bennet home in search of "the Man in the Horn-rimmed Glasses," Matt realizes Ted is unstable. Where Matt wants answers, Ted wants revenge for his wife's death, and is willing to destroy the entire town of Odessa to obtain it.

NOAH BENNET IS A COMMITTED COMPANY MAN, CONTENT WITH HIS MORALLY GRAY ROLE—UNTIL, THAT IS, HIS ADOPTIVE DAUGHTER BECOMES A TARGET. UNWILLING TO LET CLAIRE SUFFER THE FATE OF SO MANY OTHERS, HE TURNS AGAINST THE COMPANY AND RISKS HIS LIFE TO PROTECT HER AT ALL COSTS.

TAKEDOWN

After infiltrating the Company's New York facility to destroy the Walker Tracking System, Bennet finds himself facing his former mentor, Thompson. Knowing his tactical thinking, Bennet surprises Thompson before he can kill Matt Parkman, and shoots him dead.

BRINGING DOWN THE COMPANY

Over the years, there have been dozens of plots to eradicate the Company, most of which remain highly classified. Many originate with disgruntled Company operatives, including Noah Bennet, and like the Company itself, these operations, and the people behind them, are frequently morally gray in nature. Their motives range from revulsion at the organization's tactics (Mohinder Suresh and Matt Parkman) to revenge (Ted Sprague and Hana Gitelman) to self-preservation (Noah Bennet) to sinister conspiracies (Arthur Petrelli). So far, however, every blow struck against the Company has caused it to almost organically reconstitute itself.

STANDOFF
A standoff with Mohinder Suresh ends Bennet's assault on the Walker Tracking System—actually an evolved child named Molly Walker. He'll need a different approach to disconnect her from the Company.

COVER STORY
Mohinder publicly lectures on the Shanti Virus, although hardly anyone outside of the Company is paying attention. That's Mohinder's plan— to get the Company to recruit him so he can work with Noah Bennet to bring the Company down from the inside.

UNDER COVER
Mohinder's plan works—Bob Bishop comes calling, and puts him to work researching the Shanti Virus.

"JUST STAY CAREFUL AND WATCH YOUR BACK, AND YOU AND I ARE GOING TO BRING THIS WHOLE COMPANY DOWN."

WHEN CLAIRE SUDDENLY APPEARS IN HIS COMPANY PRISON CELL, NOAH QUICKLY FIGURES OUT IT IS ONE OF CANDICE'S ILLUSIONS AND AN ATTEMPT TO TRICK INFORMATION OUT OF HIM.

SYLAR

The label "serial killer" barely does justice to the disturbing Gabriel Gray. An "ordinary" watchmaker, who longs to be "special," he is profoundly altered when Dr. Chandra Suresh helps his ability surface. With it comes an insatiable hunger to take abilities from others. Adopting the name Sylar, he launches a killing spree, for which the Company must also take some culpability—they stop his suicide when he is consumed with guilt after his first kill and bait him into more butchery in order to study him. Occasionally, Sylar craves normalcy, but invariably, attempts to rehabilitate him—such as time as a Company agent—fail. Despite waves of assaults against him, his regenerative power allows the nightmare to continue.

- ■ **Power:** Intuitive Aptitude, leading to many other abilities
- ■ **Hometown:** Brooklyn, NY, but travels the world hunting victims
- ■ **Occupations:** Expert watchmaker; Company operative; but Sylar's primary endeavor is his life as a serial killer

Intuitive Aptitude

1. The ability to understand exactly how any kind of organic or mechanical system works, from basic structure to detailed operations, without any traini
2. The ability of the brain to replicate how other brains manifest evolved abil
3. It is accompanied by a "hunger" for information about how different abilit work, leading to an uncontrollable impulse to cut out the brains of victims a study them.

FATEFUL MEETING

Chandra Suresh's dogged pursuit of his so-called "Patient Zero"—the person to prove his theories correct—unintentionally unleashes the horror of Sylar on the world. Suresh gently promises to help Gray learn about his power, only to fall victim to it when the "hunger" surfaces—setting in motion events that quickly spiral out of control.

> "I JUST HAVE A TALENT FOR HOW THINGS WORK. WHERE THE PARTS SHOULD GO."

AS SYLAR GROWS STRONGER, HE PLAYS NO FAVORITES—STALKING THE WICKED ALONG WITH THE INNOCENT.

MOHINDER SURESH IS ONE OF THE FIRST TO CONFRONT SYLAR AFTER FIGURING OUT HE HAS BEEN MANIPULATING HIM. HE POISONS THE KILLER TO EXPERIMENT ON HIM,

SYLAR IS HUNTED LIKE AN ANIMAL BY THE COMPANY AND OTHERS. THEY PERIODICALLY CATCH UP TO HIM, BUT CAPTURING HIM AND HOLDING HIM PROVE TO BE

"I WANT TO BE SPECIAL. UNIQUE."

MATRICIDE

Looking for redemption, Sylar visits the woman he believes is his mother. He awes Virginia Gray with a real version of her favorite treasure—a snow globe—in her apartment. But, terrified of his powers, she becomes hysterical. His bloody response pushes Sylar irrevocably down his murderous path.

CONFRONTATION

Sylar kills his victims by telekinetically slicing open their heads to study their brains. When he attacks Peter Petrelli, he's startled to see his assault has no effect—Peter's regenerative ability heals the wound instantly.

ODD COUPLE

With guidance from Angela Petrelli, Sylar, for a time, tries to rehabilitate himself, control his hunger, and work as a Company agent. Ironically, he is paired with the man who hates him more than anyone—Noah Bennet. It won't be long before Sylar, tired of serving the agendas of others, returns to his own killing path.

SAVAGERY

Blood oozes out of the gaping head wound and limp body of mechanic Dale Smither after she is murdered by Sylar, unable to resist her special ability—enhanced hearing. Mohinder Suresh inadvertently leads Sylar right to her door on an ironic mission to warn her she could be a target.

DESPITE BEING CLOSE TO DEATH FOLLOWING HIS UNSUCCESSFUL BID TO HASTEN NEW YORK'S DESTRUCTION, SYLAR IS PERIODICALLY ASSISTED OR SAVED BY MYSTERIOUS FORCES WHO HAVE THEIR OWN AGENDAS INVOLVING HIS GREAT POWER.

ONLY ANGELA PETRELLI HAS ANY SUCCESS IN CONTROLLING SYLAR. TAKING HIM INTO CUSTODY AND CONVINCING HIM SHE IS HIS MOTHER, SHE TEACHES HIM TO CONTROL HIS WORST IMPULSES WHILE WORKING FOR THE COMPANY.

ONCE HE LEARNS HOW TO STEAL ABILITIES, SYLAR MURDERS DOZENS OF PEOPLE TO SATISFY HIS HUNGER, EVEN AFTER HE FINDS OUT HE CAN TAKE POWERS WITHOUT KILLING.

SYLAR'S POWERS

In a sense, murder is Sylar's food. His intuitive aptitude gives him the need to satiate his curiosity about how the unique abilities of genetically advanced humans work. His method of doing this is to use his telekinetic power to cleanly slice off the top of a victim's skull, exposing his or her brain. He physically interacts with the brain, "reading" and memorizing the physiological and chemical reactions that produce that individual's ability. Sylar's brain can then mimic those reactions, giving him the same power. These pages include a sampling of some of his super-powered victims. It's not comprehensive—there are doubtless other victims that have not yet been documented.

"THE KILLING. THE HUNGER. IT'S-- IRRESISTIBLE."

TELEKINESIS
The ability to move things with his mind comes from BRIAN DAVIS, Sylar's first victim from Chandra Suresh's list.

MELTING
This skill comes from ZANE TAYLOR, whom Sylar deceived by pretending to be Mohinder Suresh.

ENHANCED HEARING
This ability is taken from DALE SMITHER, and proves particularly difficult for Sylar to control at first.

EIDETIC MEMORY
Ripped from CHARLIE ANDREWS' brain at the Burnt Toast Diner, despite Hiro Nakamura's best efforts to avert it.

PRECOGNITION
Sylar takes the ability to paint the future from ISAAC MENDEZ, who bravely accepts his fate.

INDUCED RADIOACTIVITY
Sylar assaults a police transport vehicle to attack TED SPRAGUE and take his explosive power.

FLIGHT
In an alternate future, Sylar acquires the ability to fly from NATHAN PETRELLI.

ILLUSION
Sylar kills CANDICE WILLMER, but the Shanti Virus stops him from using her power.

RAPID CELL REGENERATION
CLAIRE BENNET provides this power to Sylar. She is the only victim to survive, since she can't die.

ALCHEMY
Sylar takes this skill from Company founder BOB BISHOP while infiltrating the organization's Primatech facility.

SOUND MANIPULATION
While working for the Company, Sylar can't resist killing Level 5 escapee JESSE MURPHY for this ability.

ELECTRICAL MANIPULATION
This is the first ability Sylar learns to take without killing—from ELLE BISHOP at Pinehearst. Ironically, he later murders her anyway.

ELLE BISHOP

Elle Bishop's entire life is perverted from being a Company child. Her father is founder Bob Bishop, but the organization is her true parent—from an early age she is experimented on, pushed beyond her limits, and trained, with Bob's approval, to be a ruthless operative. Ironically, her father's death frees Elle, but she is soon adrift. At Pinehearst, she finds new direction under Arthur Petrelli and an ironic relationship with her father's killer, Sylar. Together, they pursue normalcy and love, but the effort is doomed. Sylar's true nature asserts itself, and Elle's painful life ends.

- **Power: Electrical Generation and Manipulation**
- **Hometown: Odessa, TX**
- **Occupation: Longtime Company operative**

Electrical Generation and Manipulation

1. The ability to generate electricity, from sparks to over 1,000 volts.
2. The manipulation of "lightning bolts" over short and long distances.
3. Liable to become unstable, emitting arcs without control.
4. When electricity is discharged, the subject may need to "recharge" before using the ability again.

DEADLY

Desperate for her father's approval, Elle tries hard on assignments but frequently messes up. She is willing—even eager—to use deadly force. When her father assigns her to locate Peter Petrelli in Ireland, she carelessly over-reaches, to the detriment of Caitlin's brother, Ricky.

AFTER LEAVING THE COMPANY, THE ONLY HOME SHE'S EVER KNOWN, ELLE CRAVES PURPOSE—EVEN IF IT'S A DARK PURPOSE.

DYSFUNCTIONAL

Whether innate or a result of years of abuse, Elle has a sadistic streak and enjoys flirtatiously inflicting pain on Peter Petrelli. Imprisoned at the Primatech Facility—the place she calls home—he is one of the few "outsiders" she has interacted with intimately.

"I SPENT MY NINTH **BIRTHDAY** IN A GLASS ROOM WITH AN IV OF **LITHIUM** IN MY ARM AND A **SHUNT** IN THE BACK OF MY HEAD."

CLAUDE RAINS

The real name of the former Company agent dubbed "Claude Rains" (in honor of his super power) remains classified. After years in the field, Rains becomes disillusioned with the Company's methods. Risking death, he literally disappears and starts a new life, stealing essentials and training pigeons. Cynical and embittered, he shuns people and reacts violently to Peter Petrelli when he detects him. Eventually, Claude reluctantly agrees to teach Peter how to control his powers, and later, tries to do the same for Elle Bishop, with less success.

- Power: Invisibility
- Hometown: Blackpool, UK; operates out of Odessa, TX; hides in New York, NY; Last known whereabouts: London, UK
- Occupation: Former Company operative

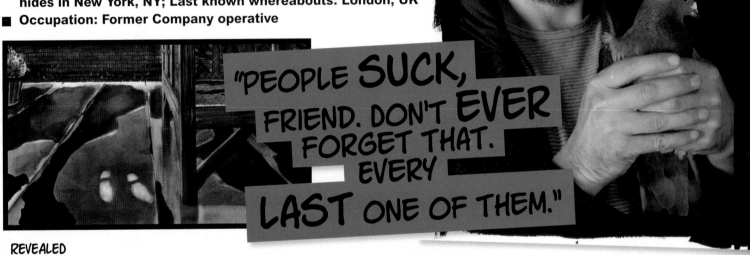

"PEOPLE SUCK, FRIEND. DON'T EVER FORGET THAT. EVERY LAST ONE OF THEM."

REVEALED

The search for Peter Petrelli, who mimics Claude's invisibility, is stymied until Isaac Mendez's painting of footsteps near the pigeon coops on the Deveaux rooftop turns up. Whether they are Peter's footprints, or Claude's, the picture illustrates that there are invisible people walking among us.

CANDICE WILLMER

Candice Willmer's ability allows her to transform her entire life into one constant illusion. Originally, she's an angry, overweight, high school outcast named Betty but suddenly, and with devastating consequences, manifests her power to alter how people perceive reality in her presence. She remakes herself into the Candice persona and is later recruited into the Company. At their behest, she has impersonated, among others, Simone Deveaux, Niki Sanders, and Sandra and Claire Bennet. Eventually, the reward for her Company service is a fatal encounter with Sylar.

- Power: Illusion
- Hometown: Clayton, NY
- Occupation: Longtime Company operative

ILLUSION OF PARADISE

Remaking herself once again—this time as a redhead named Michelle—Candice makes Sylar think he is on a beautiful tropical beach, and promises to use her ability to help him recover from his wounds. In reality, he's in a hut in Latin America with his gut delicately stitched back together. Unimpressed by her tricks, Sylar kills Candice for her power, but his injuries mean he cannot harness it.

EDEN McCAIN

Eden's life begins in abuse, descends into crime, finds new purpose with the Company at Noah Bennet's behest, and ends heroically. Abandoned by her father and abused by her stepmother, her power first manifests when she inadvertently causes the woman's death. She falls into crime before Noah recruits her to a higher purpose, and she adopts a new name, Eden. Encounters with Mohinder Suresh and Isaac Mendez make her question the Company's goals, and lead her to confront Sylar. When she is trapped by him, she takes her own life to keep her power from his grasp.

- **Power: Vocal Persuasion**
- **Hometown: Born in Utah (as Sarah Ellis), lived in LA and NYC**
- **Occupations: Thief; Book shop employee (undercover); Company operative**

Vocal Persuasion
1. The ability to persuade subjects to act upon any suggestion or idea she verbalizes as reality.
2. Eden also has the ability to cause hallucinations that appear so authentic they can lead to physical injury, or even death.

LIFE OF CRIME

Sarah Ellis is suspected of auto theft, arson, and even murder when Noah Bennet and the Haitian pluck her from her criminal ways. Her power easily deflects police officer Matt Parkman, but the Haitian is a different matter.

EDEN APPARENTLY AIDS MOHINDER IN HIS SEARCH FOR EVOLVED HUMANS, BUT SHE'S REALLY A COMPANY OPERATIVE.

DECISION TIME

Eden McCain doesn't join the Company's cause easily, spitting at Noah Bennet at one point. A gag and the presence of the Haitian mutes her vocal power, and forces her to listen to Bennet's pitch—choose punishment for her life of crime, or become a valuable force within the Company.

"I DON'T FEEL LIKE IT."

MOLLY WALKER

Although she manifested at an unusually young age, Molly Walker occupies a central role in the struggle surrounding humanity's evolution. She escapes Sylar when he murders her parents, only to be used by the Company as a living tracking device. She has a profound effect on the lives of Matt Parkman—who saves her from the "Bogeyman" Sylar—and Mohinder Suresh —who cures her of the Shanti Virus. Maury Parkman's invasion of her mind almost kills her, but she survives and faces another encounter with Sylar before going into hiding.

- **Power: Locational Clairvoyance**
- **Hometown: Los Angeles, CA; relocates to Brooklyn, NY**
- **Status: Elementary school student**

Locational Clairvoyance
1. The ability to instantly locate any living human being on Earth merely by concentrating on that person's name or image.
2. A skill harnessed by the Company to find people. Molly becomes known as the "Walker Tracking System."

SECOND FAMILY
The Company considers Molly the "Walker Tracking System" and an extremely valuable commodity. But to Matt and Mohinder, she has become a family member. They try to give her a loving and stable home life, but danger is constantly lurking.

"I JUST THINK ABOUT THEM. AND THEN I KNOW WHERE THEY ARE."

A LIVING, BREATHING TRACKING SYSTEM: THERE IS NOWHERE ON EARTH TO HIDE IF MOLLY WALKER WANTS TO FIND YOU.

THE FUTURE?
In Matt's Spirit Walk vision of what may, or may not, be his future, he sees himself married to Daphne Millbrook, raising a teenage Molly and a new baby, Daniella. In the vision, Molly's talent is used by her mother and Company associates to locate a time-traveling Peter Petrelli—a development that could lead to a major tragedy if that future comes to pass.

> "HE'S THE ONE IN MY DREAMS. HE'S THE NIGHTMARE MAN."

MATT COMES TO MOLLY'S RESCUE, AS HE DID AFTER HER PARENTS WERE KILLED, WHEN SHE IS TRAPPED INSIDE THE HALLUCINATION CREATED BY HIS FATHER, MAURY.

RESCUING MOLLY

Molly Walker becomes the focal point of a war between father and son—Maury and Matt Parkman. When Molly's ability to track people puts her in danger from Sylar and then the Company, Matt quickly takes the role of her protector and guardian. But, ironically, not even Sylar proves as terrifying to Molly as Matt's own father—Maury Parkman, a man with extremely powerful mental abilities. When Matt asks Molly to locate his father, the "Nightmare Man" responds by inducing a delusion inside her mind and leaving her body unconscious. Inside that nightmare, Matt faces down his own father. To save Molly, he stands up to Maury in the very home he was abandoned in by Maury as a child—a memory that stirs his own emotional issues and fears of

ULTIMATE DECEIT
Seemingly cornered, it's simple for Maury to convince Matt and Nathan he poses no threat but is merely a victim of the conspiracy to kill Company's founders. He produces a helix-

WORST NIGHTMARES

Maury Parkman's mind manipulations leave Matt Parkman and Nathan Petrelli locked in their worst nightmares. Matt, chasing a vision of his departed wife and unborn child, is trapped in jail. Nathan finds himself in a vicious brawl with a disfigured version of himself. Thanks to his power, Matt realizes it's not reality, and breaks the illusion.

WHEN MOLLY LOOKS FOR MAURY WITH HER POWER, HE CAN LOOK RIGHT BACK AT HER. HE INDUCES BAD DREAMS IN HER MIND AND THEN TRAPS HER INSIDE THE NIGHTMARE, LEAVING HER IN A COMA.

AWAKENING

Matt turns the tables on Maury, freeing himself and Molly, and leaving Maury apparently trapped in the dream. Molly awakens from her coma to the great relief of Matt and Mohinder.

CHARLIE ANDREWS

Charlene ("Charlie") Andrews becomes the first love of Hiro Nakamura's life, but their relationship teaches him the limitations of his power. Moments after Charlie meets Hiro at the Burnt Toast Diner, she is brutally murdered by Sylar for her power. Hiro's journey six months into the past to save her leads them to a love affair, but his attempt to change her destiny proves futile—she is destined to die, and Charlie accepts that fate with touching grace. Hiro regretfully learns that his power is not great enough to change history or decide who lives and who dies.

- **Power: Eidetic Memory**
- **Hometown: Midland, TX**
- **Occupation: Waitress at the Burnt Toast Diner**

Eidetic Memory
1. Enhanced photographic memorization capabilities, permitting total recall of words, images, and sounds with extreme accuracy—a skill Charlie first discovere[d] doing crossword puzzles.
2. The ability to fully and instantly comprehend the context and meaning of recalled information upon a single exposure to it, including new languages.

GOOGLE ON DEMAND: CHARLIE'S NATURAL CHARM ENCHANTS HER CUSTOMERS, AND SHE ENTERTAINS THEM WITH THE KNOWLEDGE OF TRIVIA MADE POSSIBLE BY HER POWER.

FATEFUL MEETING
Hiro and Ando stumble into the Burnt Toast Diner one day for lunch during their quest to save the world. At first, Charlie is merely their waitress, but her seemingly impossible ability to instantly understand Japanese, and her kind nature, draw Hiro to her. He quickly understands that, like him, Charlie is "special."

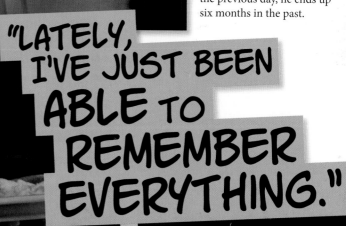

DEATH LOOMS
Sylar lurks in a corner of the Burnt Toast Diner, stalking Charlie on his way to find the nearby Claire Bennet, hungry for both women's powers. He easily assaults Charlie in the diner's kitchen, since no one was expecting him to strike there. Claire, however, will prove a more elusive quarry. Hiro detours his mission to try and save Charlie. But instead of traveling back to the previous day, he ends up six months in the past.

"LATELY, I'VE JUST BEEN ABLE TO REMEMBER EVERYTHING."

CHARLIE STANDS IN AWE AFTER HIRO MEETS HER CHALLENGE TO PRODUCE 1,000 ORIGAMI CRANES OUT OF THIN AIR, BUT SHE STILL DOESN'T FULLY UNDERSTAND HIS POWER, OR HER OWN.

"MY NAME IS HIRO NAKAMURA. I'M HERE TO SAVE YOUR LIFE."

MAGIC TIME

Hiro's attempt to save Charlie falls short, since a fatal blood clot is forming in her brain. Although she won't live long enough to fulfill her dreams and travel the world, she tells Hiro that, in their short time together, he has made her feel more alive than she ever could have imagined possible.

MESSAGE FROM THE PAST

A present-day photo of Hiro and Charlie celebrating her birthday six months ago tells Ando that his friend has made contact with her, and will eventually return.

INSTANT CHEMISTRY ERUPTS BETWEEN CHARLIE AND HIRO WHEN THEY MEET IN AT THE BURNT TOAST DINER. CHARLIE CALLS HIRO "CUTE" AND STUNS HIM WITH HER ABILITY TO SPEAK AND UNDERSTAND PERFECT JAPANESE.

CHARLIE THINKS LITTLE OF HER NEW ABILITY, CONTENT IN HER LIFE AS A SMALL-TOWN WAITRESS, BUT HIRO RECOGNIZES THAT SHE IS ANOTHER EVOLVED HUMAN, AND FEELS A DEEP AND INSTANT CONNECTION TO HER.

79

MAYA HERRERA

Maya Herrera considers her ability a curse and wants it "cured" from the moment it manifests. Appalled by all the innocent deaths she causes, she turns to her religion and other remedies in search of an end to her nightmare, but only her twin brother Alejandro can provide a measure of comfort. He helps her illegally cross the border into the United States in search of the one man who might have answers—the geneticist Chandra Suresh. After tragic involvement with both Sylar and Suresh's son, Mohinder, she finally gets the relief she seeks from Arthur Petrelli and starts a new life.

- **Power:** Poison Emission
- **Hometown:** Santo Domingo, Dominican Republic
- **Occupation:** Unknown, fugitive fleeing murder charges

Poison Emission
1. When scared or stressed, the emission of a highly poisonous black liquid from the eyes that rapidly incapacitates those in the vicinity.
2. The ability can be negated or even reversed through physical connection with the subject's brother, Alejandro.
3. Proven to be controllable with training and concentration.

MAYA HOPES THERE IS A CURE FOR HER CURSE—SHE FINDS IT HARD TO BELIEVE THAT SHE COULD BE CAPABLE OF SUCH DEADLY ACTS.

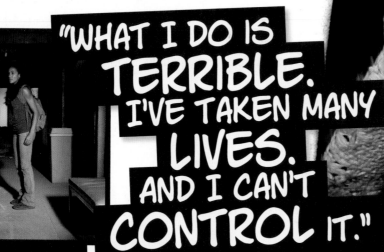

"WHAT I DO IS TERRIBLE. I'VE TAKEN MANY LIVES. AND I CAN'T CONTROL IT."

ON THE RUN
After her powers cause a tragedy, Maya and Alejandro flee the Dominican Republic and find their way to the United States in search of Chandra Suresh, whose book gives them hope that Maya can be helped. It's the start of an incredibly harrowing journey.

MOST WANTED
Maya and Alejandro are hunted as they travel from the Dominican Republic through Guatemala and Mexico. They are apprehended by police and ambushed by a border patrol, but Maya's power allows them to escape, although once again, at a heavy price.

MAYA AND ALEJANDRO ENCOUNTER SYLAR, WHO PROMISES TO HELP THEM FIND CHANDRA SURESH AFTER THEY SNEAK ACROSS THE BORDER. HIS ULTERIOR MOTIVE, HOWEVER, IS TO TAKE MAYA'S POWER.

BLACK TEARS

When Maya becomes fearful, her eyes emit a highly toxic black substance—deadly, in fact, if exposure is not quickly limited by causing Maya to stop the emission process. The effects make victims ooze the substance from their eyes, as well, and an autopsy on one victim indicates that their blood turns entirely black when poisoned by Maya. The calming effect of her brother and, later, her ability to control the process herself, mean that a handful of victims have managed to survive Maya's deadly episodes.

CALMING INFLUENCE

Until she learns to control her power, Maya can only stop her poison through physical contact with her twin, Alejandro. His eyes blacken as he appears to absorb the poison. The ability to resist, and deactivate, Maya's power appears to be Alejandro's own unique power.

DEADLY MANIFESTATION

Rage caused by her brother's new wife, Gloria, cheating on him with her ex-lover, Gilberto, on their wedding day causes Maya's power to manifest for the first time. Confronted by Gilberto after she catches them, Maya's fear triggers a deadly emission, and Gloria and Gilberto are dead moments later.

HORROR

A dazed Maya discovers her deadly onslaught is worse than she thought—not only Gloria and Gilberto are dead, but so are all the wedding guests. The only survivor is Alejandro.

SYLAR LURES MAYA INTO HIS WEB, AND SHE EVENTUALLY FALLS FOR HIM DESPITE WARNINGS FROM HER BROTHER NOT TO TRUST HIM. EVEN POWERLESS, SYLAR PROVES DEADLY AS ALEJANDRO LEARNS WHEN HE CONFRONTS THE KILLER TO PROTECT HIS SISTER.

MAYA UNWITTINGLY BECOMES INVOLVED WITH MOHINDER SURESH AT THE MOMENT THE SCIENTIST IS TURNING INTO A DANGEROUS MONSTER. STILL, HE ULTIMATELY LEADS HER TO A CURE FOR HER POWER, SO SHE CAN START A NEW LIFE.

AN ALTERNATE FUTURE

The winds of time move in circular patterns and events that haven't happened yet can be prevented, but only if someone knows they are coming. Hiro Nakamura understands the need to stop events at Kirby Plaza because he travels to the year 2011 and witnesses the draconian future that will result if the explosion happens. In this timeline, Sylar, having taken Nathan Petrelli's identity, poses as the President and hunts those with special abilities. Some evolved humans help him, including Matt Parkman, now in charge of Homeland Security, and scientist Mohinder Suresh. Hiro, Noah Bennet, and others fight back, but a cynical Peter Petrelli, harboring a terrible secret, tries to avoid the battle.

SECURITY CHIEF

Because of the massive destruction in New York, which he thinks Sylar caused, a future Matt Parkman believes he is doing the right thing in serving the government's aggression against super-powered individuals. Thus, as the head of Homeland Security, he mercilessly tracks them down.

THIS ISAAC MENDEZ PAINTING SHOWS NATHAN PETRELLI IN THE OVAL OFFICE, SERVING AS PRESIDENT OF THE UNITED STATES. HOWEVER, AS WITH MANY OF ISAAC'S PAINTINGS, ITS MEANING IS NOT IMMEDIATELY CLEAR. IS HE PREDICTING NATHAN'S ASCENSION TO THE PRESIDENCY, OR HINTING THAT SYLAR WILL IMPERSONATE HIM IN THE ROLE?

FUTURE HIRO
Present-day Hiro gets guidance on changing history from his future self—a fierce opponent of the government crackdown who has been labeled a terrorist. Future Hiro unhesitatingly gives his life to help his present-day counterpart rectify past events.

CONFLICTED
Mohinder Suresh accepts the government's moves against those with powers, but reluctantly. Years of scientific research convince him there is no other way to protect society from dangerous individuals, but when he learns more aggressive measures are planned, he helps Hiro escape, hoping he can change this fate.

"JESSICA"
In 2011, Niki Sanders works as a stripper named Jessica, trying to mask her own pain about Micah's death and ease the suffering of her lover, Peter Petrelli.

"SANDRA"
Like many evolved humans in 2011, Claire Bennet hides, working as a waitress named Sandra at the Burnt Toast Diner. Events out of her control, however, will soon lead to her worst nightmare—Sylar.

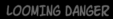

LOOMING DANGER
One thing unchanged in the future is Noah Bennet's concern for Claire. He comes to help her escape before authorities arrive, but Claire has fallen in love and resists.

RELUCTANT
Hiro Nakamura begs Peter Petrelli to use his power to help eradicate the timeline that transforms his future life into a living hell. Burdened by knowledge that he caused the tragedy in New York—not Sylar as is popularly believed—Peter reluctantly agrees to join the fight.

ESCAPE ROUTE
Noah Bennet helps evolved refugees escape government detection. His pact with Matt Parkman means he turns dangerous individuals over to Homeland Security in return for anonymity for the others, but it all goes wrong when Matt betrays Noah.

IN A TEMPORAL PARADOX, PRESENT-DAY HIRO MEETS HIS FUTURE SELF. IT TAKES TWO HIROS TOGETHER TO TRY AND CHANGE THE TERRIBLE FATE AWAITING NEW YORK.

"THIS IS A MAP OF TIME. THE EVENTS THAT LED UP TO THE BOMB THAT DESTROYED HALF THIS CITY."

STRING MAP
In the future, Hiro marvels at the elaborate time map he discovers in Isaac Mendez's loft. Ironically, he learns that he is, or rather will be, responsible for its creation.

STRING THEORY

Five years after New York's destruction on November 8, 2006, Hiro Nakamura constructs a time map out of string connecting the people and events related to the tragedy. The map indicates that the key to averting the disaster is saving Claire Bennet's life, and tells him the best moment in time to task Peter Petrelli with that mission. When he returns to his own time, though, nothing has changed. His younger self arrives, and Future Hiro learns he failed to kill Sylar. Now, Present-day Hiro must try again.

TWO HIROS

Witnessing mass destruction and the death of his best friend, Ando, casts a shadow over Future Hiro's life, deeply hardening his previously sunny disposition. Present-day Hiro's outlook is also darkened when he sees what the future might hold, making his mission all the more critical.

"I NEED TO GET YOU BACK THERE. ON THE DAY THE BOMB EXPLODES, YOU HAVE TO KILL SYLAR."

MISSION IMPERATIVE

Hiro originally fails to kill Sylar because the murderer had taken Claire's regenerative power, so he asks his present-day self to correct that error. Of course, not even his time map is 100 percent accurate. Sylar is, indeed, deadly, but his role at Kirby Plaza isn't exactly as the time map appears to suggest.

PETER LYING DEAD?

While Peter Petrelli is pondering the "Save the cheerleader, save the world" message he got from Future Hiro, Isaac Mendez's prophetic painting turns up. The image provides a clue of where to find the cheerleader, but also foretells Peter's death. Nathan Petrelli, in an attempt to save his brother's life, destroys the painting so Peter will never see it. However, Simone Deveaux shows Peter a copy because, although she doesn't want to lose him, she loves him enough to understand his need to fulfill his destiny. On seeing the image, Peter leaps into action and leaves for Texas, even though he believes it may mean his death, as prophesied. The image doesn't reveal he will survive using Claire's unique healing ability.

SAVE THE CHEERLEADER,
SAVE THE WORLD

It begins with a cryptic message from the future about the fate of a teenage girl. That girl—Claire Bennet—can't be killed, and this ability puts her at the center of the war for humanity's fate. The killer Sylar targets her, craving her immortality. With that ability, Sylar will, in fact, destroy New York, according to prophetic paintings from Isaac Mendez and events glimpsed five years into one alternate future. A future Hiro Nakamura realizes Sylar must not acquire Claire's ability. Thus, he sends a frantic message reverberating through time—save Claire at all costs.

THE MESSAGE

Future Hiro travels five years into the past to deliver a message designed save Claire and millions of others. It's delivered on a dark subway train, frozen in time by Hiro, to a

PROPHECY

Isaac Mendez creates paintings predicting an attack upon a high school cheerleader by a menacing figure. They appear to document Sylar's future attack on Claire, but like many Mendez works, they don't tell the entire story, such as whether the cheerleader pictured is, in fact, Claire Bennet, to begin with.

RESCUE ATTEMPT

Peter arrives at Union Wells High School in Odessa, Texas, as Homecoming festivities get underway, hoping to fulfill his mission to save the cheerleader's life. Even now, however, he still doesn't understand who he is saving, or what he is up against.

THE ASSAULT

As Claire senses something is wrong and seeks a path to safety for herself and her rival cheerleader, Jackie Wilcox, Sylar silently stalks the girl's

DEADLY ENCOUNTER

On Homecoming evening, Peter heroically faces off with Sylar even though he has no idea that his ability to mimic the powers of others could enable him to survive the encounter. At 8:12 p.m., he lies bleeding on cold concrete after falling from the stadium bleachers while tangling with Sylar in his effort to save Claire Bennet.

IMPOSSIBLE RECOVERY

Claire watches in amazement as Peter gingerly sits up, somehow alive despite his deadly fall and extensive injuries. Before Claire's eyes, Peter begins to heal —exhibiting Claire's regenerative ability, which his body emulates without his realizing it.

AFTERMATH

Events are a blur for Peter in the wake of his encounter with Sylar. As police take him into custody, he is shocked by his body's sudden healing power. He watches Claire escape, wonders about Sylar's fate, and struggles to comprehend what is happening to him. Police officer Matt Parkman reads Peter's mind to determine that he is not the mysterious Sylar.

CAPTURED

Sylar escapes the police after his attempt to kill Claire goes awry, but Company agents Eden McCain and the Haitian succeed in apprehending him. The Company's plan, under Noah Bennet's direction, is to experiment on Sylar to learn more about his genetic abilities, since he is the first evolved human the Company has ever encountered to possess more than one super power. However, Eden's grudge against him will eventually lead to Sylar's escape.

EXPLODING
MAN

Isaac Mendez believes that his ability to paint the future only works when he's high on heroin, but he's trying to quit for his girlfriend Simone Deveaux. Noah Bennet, desperate for clues about the future so he can keep Claire safe, kidnaps Isaac and uses Eden McCain's powers of persuasion to force him to shoot up. The result is this image of an exploding man—finally the source of the future nuclear explosion in New York is known. However, the painting gives no clue as to the identity of the person. In the days that follow, three people with the ability to explode emerge: Ted Sprague, Sylar, and Peter Petrelli. Any one of them could be responsible.

HOW DO YOU STOP AN
EXPLODING MAN?

Daniel Linderman and his colleagues believe that sacrificing New York—less than 0.7 percent of the world's population—in a massive explosion is an acceptable sacrifice for a greater good—a catalyst for major change. Out of the chaos, they expect people will unite in their fear, and look to a strong leader to protect them—Nathan Petrelli. With Nathan installed in the White House, Linderman and his associates will have the ultimate power. Early on, the event appears a foregone conclusion—predicted by Isaac Mendez and seen happening in the future by Hiro Nakamura. However, events at Kirby Plaza take an unexpected turn as Nathan chooses a different role for himself.

THE MOMENT ARRIVES

Linderman's weapon of choice is Peter Petrelli, who is unable to control the radioactive power he gained from Ted Sprague. At Kirby Plaza, Peter comprehends, to his horror, the reality of Isaac Mendez's prophecy. The explosive energy is percolating within him and barring a miracle, he, and millions of others, will soon be dead.

HIRO ARRIVES TO FULFILL HIS DESTINY BY PLUNGING HIS SWORD INTO SYLAR'S CHEST.

HIRO'S ATTACK LEAVES SYLAR BARELY ALIVE. HE SUCCUMBS, CONTENT THAT HIS GOAL OF SEEING THE CITY DESTROYED WILL SOON BE FULFILLED.

PETER PETRELLI CONFRONTS SYLAR AT KIRBY PLAZA, WITH NEW YORK'S FATE HANGING IN THE BALANCE. WHEN IT BECOMES CLEAR THAT PETER IS ACTUALLY THE EXPLODING MAN IN ISAAC MENDEZ'S PAINTING, SYLAR TAUNTS HIM, CALLING HIM THE TRUE VILLAIN—SOMEONE WHO WILL BE RESPONSIBLE FOR MORE DEATHS THAN SYLAR EVER WILL.

OPPOSITION

As New York's destruction moves closer to fruition, forces align to stop it. Thanks to Hiro and Ando's visits to the future and Isaac's ability to paint the future, Linderman's planned massacre becomes the obsession of people willing to risk everything to stop it. Isaac, Hiro, Ando, Peter, Noah, Claire, Niki, D.L., Molly, and Matt unite to try and avert the cataclysmic event.

AFTERMATH

When all appears lost, Nathan steps forward to change history and his own destiny. Moments before Peter detonates, Nathan flies him high above the city, where the explosion takes place, saving millions. Four months later, though, Nathan is confused by his survival and haunted by visions of his own, horribly scarred visage. Peter is presumed dead, Nathan's wife and children have left, his political career is over, and confusion fogs his mind.

NOAH TRIES TO SHOOT PETER, BUT BECAUSE OF SYLAR'S ATTACK, HE CAN'T MOVE.

CLAIRE IS UNDER INSTRUCTIONS FROM PETER TO SHOOT HIM IF HE IS ABOUT TO EXPLODE.

D.L., NIKI, MICAH, AND MOLLY WATCH IN AWE AS PETER DETONATES HIGH OVER NEW YORK CITY.

THE SHANTI VIRUS

A s humans evolve, so do organisms capable of attacking them on the cellular level. Case in point: the Shanti Virus—named after its first known victim, Shanti Suresh. The original strain is fatal but only threatens evolved humans—an early symptom is the blunting of their abilities. The virus becomes a major focus of those researching evolution, including Chandra and Mohinder Suresh, as well as Company scientists, who develop multiple strains capable of stripping abilities or even killing. One mutated strain is developed, however, that goes too far—the so-called Strain 138, a virus which is highly contagious and incredibly destructive.

"THE VIRUS HAS MUTATED. IT'S IMMUNE."

ORIGINAL HOST

Shanti Suresh (pictured aged 5 with her parents), Mohinder's deceased older sister, is the first known victim of the virus. As the original strain attacks only evolved humans, Shanti probably would have manifested powers. Her father, Chandra, correctly predicted that antibodies in a sibling's blood would neutralize the virus, but Mohinder was born too late to save Shanti.

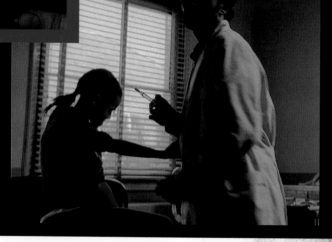

MORAL QUANDARY

After infiltrating the Company, Mohinder Suresh faces a dilemma—inject Monica Dawson with an experimental strain of the virus on instructions from Bob Bishop and maintain his cover, or refuse and risk being exposed. This unnamed strain was developed by the Company—one of possibly dozens of versions less deadly than Strain 138 that still exist—to simply eliminate abilities from evolved people without killing them. But it has never been tested, and Mohinder refuses to endanger Monica.

WHEN MOLLY WALKER IS THE SECOND VICTIM OF THE ORIGINAL STRAIN, MOHINDER DOES WHAT NO-ONE COULD DO FOR HIS SISTER—HE USES HIS OWN BLOOD TO CURE HER.

MOHINDER TRAVELS TO HAITI TO TREAT THE THIRD KNOWN VICTIM— THE HAITIAN. HE CURES HIM, BUT WORRIES ABOUT THE VIRUS' ABILITY TO TRAVEL GREAT DISTANCES.

TORMENTED BY VISIONS PUT IN HER MIND BY MAURY PARKMAN, NIKI SANDERS CONTEMPLATES USING THE VIRUS TO KILL BOB BISHOP. FIGHTING MAURY'S INFLUENCE HOWEVER, SHE INSTEAD INJECTS HERSELF WITH A MUTATED STRAIN RESISTANT TO MOHINDER'S CURE.

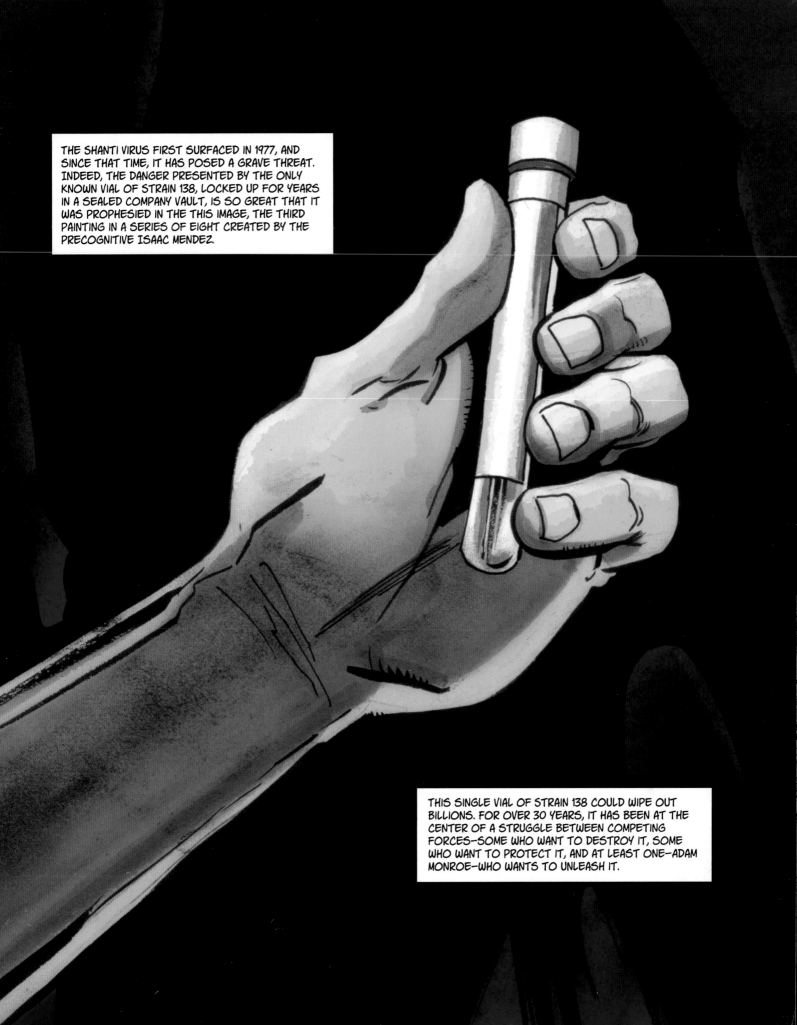

THE SHANTI VIRUS FIRST SURFACED IN 1977, AND SINCE THAT TIME, IT HAS POSED A GRAVE THREAT. INDEED, THE DANGER PRESENTED BY THE ONLY KNOWN VIAL OF STRAIN 138, LOCKED UP FOR YEARS IN A SEALED COMPANY VAULT, IS SO GREAT THAT IT WAS PROPHESIED IN THE THIS IMAGE, THE THIRD PAINTING IN A SERIES OF EIGHT CREATED BY THE PRECOGNITIVE ISAAC MENDEZ.

THIS SINGLE VIAL OF STRAIN 138 COULD WIPE OUT BILLIONS. FOR OVER 30 YEARS, IT HAS BEEN AT THE CENTER OF A STRUGGLE BETWEEN COMPETING FORCES—SOME WHO WANT TO DESTROY IT, SOME WHO WANT TO PROTECT IT, AND AT LEAST ONE—ADAM MONROE—WHO WANTS TO UNLEASH IT.

SHOT in the EYE

Isaac Mendez's final painting in a series of eight foreshadows Noah Bennet's death, but it doesn't tell the whole story. Noah is shot by his co-conspirator in bringing down the Company, Mohinder Suresh, when the exchange of the hostages, Claire Bennet and Elle Bishop, goes awry. However, despite a fatal bullet to the head, this is not the end for Noah. Mohinder saves him from certain death using the healing properties in Claire's blood. The image is also shocking to Bennet because it looks as though Claire is enjoying an embrace with a man while her father lies dying, but in fact she is being restrained by West, hysterical with grief.

7/8

8/8

THE PRICE OF **BLOOD**

As the Shanti Virus mutates and works its way into the population, it becomes increasingly clear to Mohinder Suresh that the vaccine he created from his own blood is no longer effective. Looking for new solutions, he becomes convinced that combining his vaccine with the regenerative properties of Claire Bennet's blood could save millions of lives. Thus, he reluctantly agrees to Company man Bob Bishop's demand that he partner with Elle Bishop to kidnap Claire. They succeed and take some blood from Claire, but it comes at a high price. The action leads to another kidnapping and a hostage exchange that goes awry—with devastating consequences for all involved.

PRECIOUS BLOOD
Bob extracts blood from Claire to aid the Company's Shanti Virus research project, but the action will have consequences both positive and negative. It will save Noah Bennet, and possibly many others, but it also gives renewed, deadly strength to Sylar.

HARDBALL
Driven to ruthlessness to protect Claire, Noah Bennet retaliates by grabbing Bob's daughter, Elle. In order to incapacitate her powers, he binds her feet in water—every time she uses her ability, she shocks herself.

ON TARGET
As West flies off with Claire safely in his arms, Elle unleashes a surgical lightning bolt that knocks them out of the sky, triggering chaos and retaliation.

"YOU TOUCH MY DAUGHTER AND I'LL KILL YOURS."

HEALING PROPERTIES
By rights, he should be dead after being shot in the eye. Instead, Noah Bennet miraculously recovers in a nondescript Company hospital room—saved, ironically, by the healing blood forcibly taken from his daughter.

NOAH DECIDES TO EXECUTE BOB TO DEAL THE COMPANY A MORTAL BLOW. MOHINDER BELIEVES THAT WOULD PREVENT HIM FROM CURING THE SHANTI VIRUS, AND SO HE RESOLVES TO STOP BENNET.

THIS, THE SEVENTH OF EIGHT PROPHETIC ISAAC MENDEZ PAINTINGS, SHOWS THE RESULT OF MOHINDER'S AGONIZING CHOICE: SHOOT NOAH OR RISK FORGOING HIS CHANCE TO CURE THE SHANTI VIRUS.

OUT FOR BLOOD

Claire's blood interests many people, including Sylar, who lost his powers after being stabbed by Hiro. He takes Molly hostage, knowing Mohinder will bring what he craves to save her.

TEST CASE

Sylar experiments on Maya. He viciously attacks her and orders Mohinder to restore her with the blood. Seeing her recovery, he injects it into himself, restoring his lost powers—Sylar is back.

"THERE'S A STORM COMING, DR. SURESH."

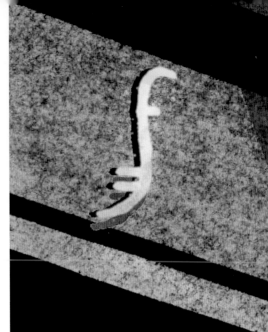

PETER and CAITLIN in MONTREAL

Peter Petrelli awakes in a cargo crate in Ireland with no memory of who he is or even that he has special powers. He becomes involved with a gang of local criminals and falls for an Irish woman, Caitlin. Convinced he is destined for something important, he is seized by the urge to paint. Without knowing it, he uses Isaac Mendez's precognitive ability and creates this image of himself and Caitlin in Montreal, a place he's never been before. Combined with two plane tickets he found to Montreal, the painting makes him think it is an instruction he must follow. Behind the door on Boulevard Saint-Laurent, Peter finds a man called Adam Monroe, his real identity, and a mission to save the world from a deadly virus—but all is not quite as it seems.

DESPITE KNOWING MORE THAN ANYONE ABOUT THE DANGERS OF STRAIN 138, PETER PETRELLI INADVERTENTLY COMES VERY CLOSE TO HELPING ADAM MONROE MAKE THOSE HORRORS A REALITY.

ESCAPE

While they are imprisoned at a Company facility, Adam gradually earns Peter's trust. He convinces Peter that he is needed to help stop a Shanti Virus pandemic. Peter eventually uses his power to help them both break out of the facility.

DESTROYING THE VIRUS

O ver the years, the Company experiments with various mutations of the Shanti Virus. In 1977, a single vial of the most virulent form—Strain 138—is developed by scientist Victoria Pratt. When she recognizes the threat it poses, she demands it be destroyed, and leaves the Company, horrified at what she has created. That's when Adam Monroe becomes obsessed with acquiring the vial to unleash the virus on the world in order to "cure" it. He first tries in 1977, but is foiled by the Company founders, who imprison him. Decades later, he grabs an opportunity to trick Peter Petrelli into helping him escape prison and track down and steal Strain 138 so he can release it. But he doesn't count on Hiro Nakamura, Nathan Petrelli, Matt Parkman—and Peter—standing in his way.

CONFUSION

After escaping the Company, Peter finds himself cornered again—this time by the Haitian, who traps him in a cargo container headed for Ireland. His mind is wiped clean of his past, his abilities, and the looming virus threat.

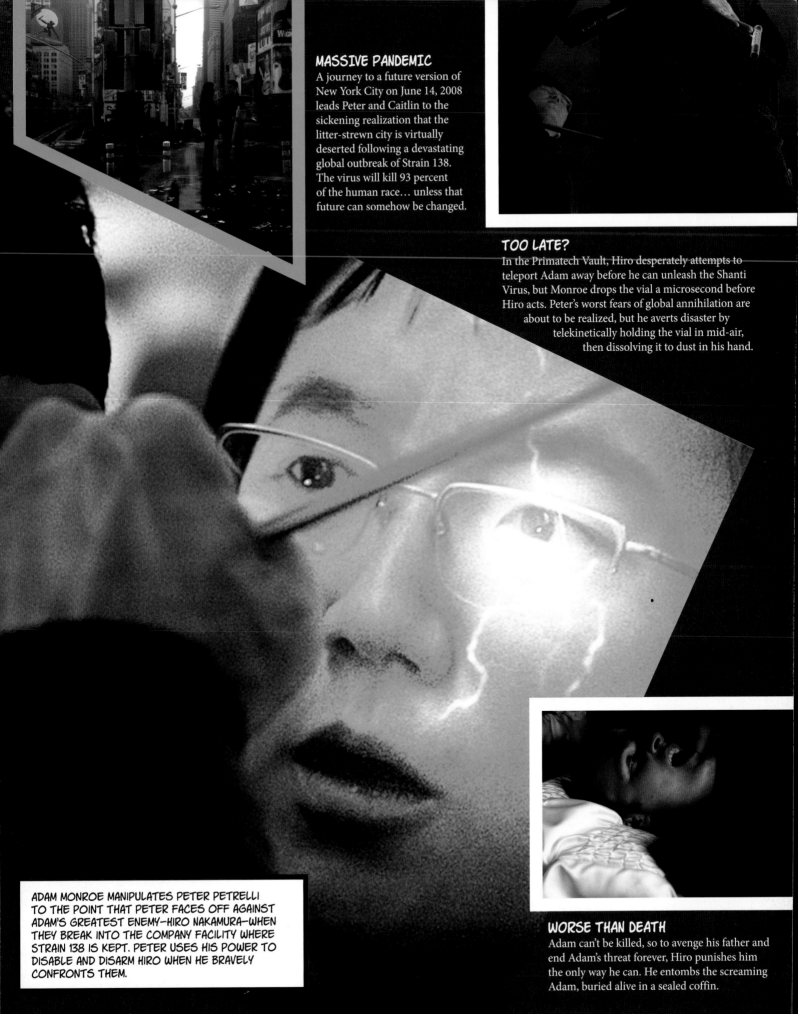

MASSIVE PANDEMIC

A journey to a future version of New York City on June 14, 2008 leads Peter and Caitlin to the sickening realization that the litter-strewn city is virtually deserted following a devastating global outbreak of Strain 138. The virus will kill 93 percent of the human race… unless that future can somehow be changed.

TOO LATE?

In the Primatech Vault, Hiro desperately attempts to teleport Adam away before he can unleash the Shanti Virus, but Monroe drops the vial a microsecond before Hiro acts. Peter's worst fears of global annihilation are about to be realized, but he averts disaster by telekinetically holding the vial in mid-air, then dissolving it to dust in his hand.

ADAM MONROE MANIPULATES PETER PETRELLI TO THE POINT THAT PETER FACES OFF AGAINST ADAM'S GREATEST ENEMY—HIRO NAKAMURA—WHEN THEY BREAK INTO THE COMPANY FACILITY WHERE STRAIN 138 IS KEPT. PETER USES HIS POWER TO DISABLE AND DISARM HIRO WHEN HE BRAVELY CONFRONTS THEM.

WORSE THAN DEATH

Adam can't be killed, so to avenge his father and end Adam's threat forever, Hiro punishes him the only way he can. He entombs the screaming Adam, buried alive in a sealed coffin.

TRACY STRAUSS

Tracy Strauss spends most of her life unaware of her origins, her identical sisters Niki and Barbara, and her power. She only manifests after becoming a political operative and an associate of Nathan Petrelli. Her power accidentally causes a death, triggering a suicide attempt by Tracy, but Nathan saves her, and they begin a romantic relationship. After investigating her past, still pursuing political power, she nudges Nathan toward Pinehearst. When it fails, they separate, but she is soon targeted as a threat and detained along with other super-powered people.

- **Power: Freezing (synthetically induced before birth)**
- **Hometown: Beverly Hills, CA; relocates to Washington D.C.**
- **Occupations: Political adviser to Governor Robert Malden; Aide to Senator Nathan Petrelli; Lobbyist for Pinehearst**

Freezing
1. The ability to reduce the temperature of matter with touch.
2. It was synthetically given to Tracy before birth by the Company.
3. Freezing at maximum level can cause matter to become brittle and shatter.
4. As Tracy appears to retain her own body heat, it is likely that she absorbs heat out of matter, rather than emitting cold.

"THIS ABILITY. I'VE HURT PEOPLE."

AT ONE POINT TRACY IS SUICIDAL, AND YET, SOON AFTER, SHE'S STRATEGICALLY JOCKEYING FOR POWER IN THE WORLD OF THE GENETICALLY EVOLVED.

FATEFUL ATTRACTION
Tracy Strauss' relationship with Nathan is massively consequential. She helps him become Senator, they save each other's lives, and they become entangled together at Pinehearst. However, she never loses her attraction to power and when her plan to join Pinehearst's success falls apart, she abandons Nathan after they disagree over their next move. That looming move, by Nathan, will devastate their relationship.

MYSTERY SISTER
Tracy sees a photo of her triplet, Barbara, when she investigates her past and visits former Company scientist Dr. Zimmerman, but she never learns Barbara's fate.

SLOWING DOWN

In a Berlin theater, Hiro and Ando briefly catch up to Daphne as they find their powers blunted by the Haitian. She teases them, even as they plot to grab the other half of the Formula using guile in lieu of their powers.

TOO FAST

Daphne officially becomes Hiro Nakamura's "nemesis" the day she invades his office at Yamagato Industries. Her speed trail sends papers flying, except for the one paper she grabs from Hiro's hands as she knocks him down—Kaito Nakamura's half of the ultra-dangerous Formula she will bring to Arthur Petrelli. Before Hiro realizes what happened, she is gone.

"I WORK FOR A GUY. I FIND STUFF. HE PAYS ME. SIMPLE AS THAT."

DAPHNE MILLBROOK

The manifestation of Daphne Millbrook's "speedster" power completely transforms her life. Suffering until then from cerebral palsy, her transformation lets her escape her home and become a world-class thief. In that role, she gathers pieces of the Formula for Arthur Petrelli, thinking of herself as a harmless thief just looking for quick scores. But when she discovers she's been pulled into life and death matters, she's troubled. Matt Parkman's selfless nature and conviction they belong together eventually win her over, and she becomes a hero at last—working to stop Pinehearst and eliminate the Formula once and for all.

DAPHNE'S HESITATION TO TRUST ANYONE, AND HER DREAD OF ARTHUR, ARE DRIVEN BY HER FEAR OF BEING HELPLESS AGAIN.

- **Power: Superhuman Speed**
- **Hometown: Lawrence, KS; relocates briefly to Paris, France**
- **Occupations: Master thief; Pinehearst agent**

Superhuman Speed
1. Ability to move at several hundred miles an hour—exact speed is undocumented.
2. She can move objects and at least one person with her through physical contact.
3. She appears to move at normal speed when time is frozen, and leaves behind a colorful, detectable "speed trail" as time slows down.
4. When enhanced by the power of Ando Masahashi, she is able to move through time.

USUTU

Even after his apparent death, mysteries linger regarding the African Shaman Usutu. He's certainly an evolved human with the same power of precognition that Isaac Mendez possesses, but he's more than that. His power also encompasses ancient practices of his African forefathers. Beyond his prophetic paintings, he has the ability to guide others, such as Matt Parkman and Hiro Nakamura, into seeing their own destinies. Indeed, even after Arthur Petrelli kills him, Usutu continues appearing in Parkman's telepathic trances. Did Usutu, like Isaac, permit his own death to achieve something greater? Was Usutu really killed, or has he merely taken another form? Why, of all places, did Future Peter dump Parkman in Usutu's backyard? Only time will tell if these questions get answered.

- **Power:** Precognition
- **Home:** Botswana, Africa
- **Occupation:** African Shaman

Precognition
1. Like Isaac Mendez, he is able to paint or draw details of the future.
2. The ability requires a trance-like state, in which he is unaware of the environment around him.
3. Even after death, seems to be able to act as a spirit guide to others, via dreams and encounters, possibly like Sanjog Iyer.

"YOU MUST FIND YOUR TOTEM. IT WILL GUIDE YOU ON YOUR JOURNEY."

RIDDLES
Stranded in the African desert, Matt Parkman's life turns suddenly when he encounters Usutu, who appears to know him better than he knows himself. The Shaman feeds his body and mind, using his prophetic paintings and wisdom to give Matt a glimpse into his destiny —alongside that of Daphne Millbrook.

WHATEVER HIS MYSTERIES, USUTU HAS A CLEARER UNDERSTANDING OF HIS COGNITIVE ABILITIES THAN ISAAC MENDEZ.

SPIRIT GUIDE
Using an ancient recipe, Usutu concocts a hallucinogenic, paste-like substance that, when consumed by others, can put them into dream-like precognitive trances. In this way, Usutu sends Hiro Nakamura on a Spirit Walk, opening the door for him to learn the truth about Arthur Petrelli and what he must do to stop him.

KNOX STARTS AS A HARD-CORE CRIMINAL, BUT FINDS GREATER PURPOSE WORKING TOWARD ARTHUR PETRELLI'S VISION OF THE FUTURE.

KNOX

Benjamin "Knox" Washington grows up on crime-infested streets, and the manifestation of his power launches him into a lawless spree that brings him to the Company's attention. Apprehended by Noah Bennet, his burning desire for revenge festers during his time incarcerated in Level 5. When the inmates escape, Knox dominates a group that goes on a new crime spree. His agenda, though, is no longer self-enrichment—he wants to finally settle accounts with Bennet. Sylar ruins his plans, but Knox gets away and soon finds a purpose he feels matches his great power—to help Arthur Petrelli achieve world dominance. This time, though, Peter Petrelli gets in the way.

- **Power: Superhuman Strength, fueled by the fears of others**
- **Hometown: Watts, Greater Los Angeles, CA**
- **Occupations: Gang leader; Escapee from Level 5; Pinehearst agent**

"IT WAS NOT JUST ABOUT THE MONEY. IN FACT, IT WAS MOSTLY ABOUT REVENGE."

RIGHT-HAND MAN
As Arthur Petrelli's most trusted thug, Knox goes after anyone and everyone, supremely confident since his enemy's fear fuels his strength. When Arthur dies, he's not comfortable following Nathan Petrelli and rebels.

TOUGH GUY
Flint has long lived the thug life—actually enjoying hurting anyone who opposes him or his friends. On the other hand, he's extremely loyal to his sister and his fellow Level 5 escapees.

FLINT

Flint Gordon grew up in foster homes, with little education or guidance, and until Level 5, he had only one meaningful relationship—with his older sister, Meredith Gordon. They share the power of pyrokinesis, and for years, Meredith protected him, no matter what. But when he's captured and placed in Level 5, he quickly bonds with fellow thug Knox, and sticks with him when both are recruited into the Pinehearst Company. After Arthur Petrelli's death, they break with Nathan Petrelli, and when Flint attacks Nathan, Tracy Strauss takes him out of play, using ice pre-emptively against his fire power.

- **Power: Pyrokinesis**
- **Hometown: Rural Arkansas; relocates to Texas**
- **Occupations: Career criminal; Escapee from Level 5;**

USUTU'S PAINTINGS

Usutu, an African precog, paints images of people and places half a world away. They are visions of the future, although the events shown appear not to be set in stone. Rather, they are starting points within the timeline, subject to interpretation and they change depending on current events. When Future Peter goes back in time to shoot his brother, as predicted by Usutu, he plans only to stop Nathan from revealing the truth about super-powered humans because he has witnessed the dystopic society this will create in the future, but unimagined consequences result. Events predicted by Usutu cease to be and new ones emerge, splitting time, creating multiple potential outcomes, and putting not just the town of Costa Verde but the whole of the planet in danger.

STEPHEN CANFIELD

Stephen's formidable ability—creating powerful vortexes that make things disappear forever—destroys his life. His inability to control it early on turns a disagreement with a neighbor into tragedy. Branded a dangerous killer, Canfield is grabbed by the Company, leaving his wife, Elizabeth, and children abandoned. Escaping two years later, he only wants to find his family, but terrified of his power, they reject him. When the Company tracks him down, Noah Bennet gives him a way out—make Sylar disappear and walk free. But, Canfield refuses to be a cold-blooded murderer, and instead disappears in a vortex.

- **Power: Gravitational Vortex Creation**
- **Hometown: New York City, NY; relocates to Los Angeles, CA**
- **Occupation: Used car salesman; Escapee from Level 5**

MISUNDERSTOOD

When Claire Bennet strikes out on her own to hunt bad guys, Stephen is her first target. However, hearing his story, she identifies with his struggle and begins to doubt her father's perspective. She falters further when she sees Noah burst in, partnered with the killer she hates—Sylar.

ESCAPE

During Sylar's invasion of the Company, Elle Bishop loses control and shuts down the electrical grid, allowing detainees with dangerous super powers to escape Level 5. Among them are Flint Gordon, Knox, Stephen Canfield, the German, Jesse Murphy, and Eric Doyle. Rounding them up has been a Company priority ever since.

THE GERMAN

The man known only as "the German" terrorizes European financial institutions for years by using his magnetic ability to rip apart steel bank vaults. He is eventually taken down by a Company operation that succeeds despite the fact that a mole inside the Company tips him off. Before capture, he uses his power to stop bullets shooting from an agent's gun and sends them back, killing the agent instantly. The German is held at Level 5 security until escaping during the massive breakout. He joins Knox and others in robbing a bank, cruelly killing civilians in cold blood, but eventually challenges Knox—an error that costs his life.

- **Power: Magnetism**
- **Hometown: Munich, Germany**
- **Occupation: Bank robber; Escapee from Level 5**

JESSE MURPHY

Jesse Murphy is a genetically advanced thug who, one day, meets a fellow evolved human—Benjamin "Knox" Washington—and joins him on a crime spree that lasts until Noah Bennet and the Haitian force them into Level 5. There, Jesse remains until the day of the big breakout, but by then, the consciousness of the present-day version of Peter Petrelli has been forced into Jesse's body by Future Peter. During a bank robbery, Peter is finally released, and the real Jesse assaults Noah. Sylar stops him and, unable to resist his power, murders Jesse.

- **Power: Sound Manipulation—voice generates fatal sound waves**
- **Hometown: Las Vegas, NV; relocates to Los Angeles, CA**
- **Occupation: Runner at the Corinthian Casino; Gang member; Criminal; Escapee from Level 5**

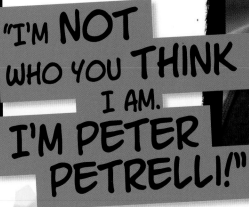

TWISTED IDENTITY
Peter accompanies Flint Gordon on the bank robbery, but the world only sees Jesse. Instead of fleeing, Peter decides to stay close to the villains, hoping to prevent them from killing anyone.

> "I'M **NOT** WHO YOU **THINK** I AM. I'M PETER PETRELLI!"

ERIC DOYLE

After being orphaned at the age of five, Eric Doyle is raised by his uncle until the day the man mocks him. Eric's ability manifests, and he makes his uncle swim out to sea until he drowns. Getting away with it after the death was ruled accidental, Doyle becomes emboldened and begins using his power maliciously to control people who he feels slight him. Among his victims will be Claire Bennet and her real and adopted moms.

- **Power: Puppetmaster—controls the movements of others**
- **Hometown: Omaha, NE; relocates to Costa Verde, CA**
- **Occupations: Owner of Doyle's Marionette Theatre; Escapee from Level 5**

PUPPETIZED
Doyle developed an obsession with Meredith Gordon when they first met at a flea market. Years later, he victimizes her again, determined to make her appear to love him. When Claire and Sandra Bennet go to rescue her from his clutches, they are forced into a demented game of Russian Roulette.

PINEHEARST

To the outside world, New Jersey's Pinehearst Company is a progressive, cutting-edge, biotechnology company focused on scientific solutions to the world's problems. In reality, it is headquarters for Arthur Petrelli's organization as he plots to create and use a special Formula designed to develop a race of genetically enhanced humans. Inside the facility, Mohinder labors to test and perfect the Formula—work protected by the team of super-powered humans Arthur has assembled. After Arthur's death, Nathan takes over, convinced that super-powered armies are necessary to protect the world. However, many think his plan will result in the opposite outcome, and by the time the battle ends, both Pinehearst and the Company are razed to the ground.

FAMILY LEGACY

Arthur pictured with his sons, Peter and Nathan, in happier times. Even then, he was plotting to launch Pinehearst. Years later, it will be the site of the family's disintegration—Arthur will be killed by Sylar, and the brothers will choose opposite sides in the battle for humanity's fate.

COMING TOGETHER

Prophesied by Usutu to fall in love and marry, Matt Parkman and Daphne Millbrook meet when she is instructed to recruit him to Pinehearst. Ironically, Matt brings her over to the opposite cause and they join the battle to stop Arthur and Nathan Petrelli.

"THEY WANT TO CREATE A WORLD FILLED WITH DANGEROUS PEOPLE."

SEEKING CLUES

When Arthur Petrelli wipes Hiro Nakamura's mind, the process leaves Hiro with only the memories he had when he was 10 years old. In a Tokyo comic book store, Ando Masahashi flips through a copy of Isaac Mendez's *9th Wonders!* comic book seeking clues on how to restore his friend, but instead, he learns another eclipse is looming. Later, the pair gets help from comic geeks in piecing together the various predictions found in back issues of *9th Wonders!*. Eventually, they figure out that the eclipse will temporarily remove everyone's special powers.

THE FORMULA

Mohinder's gruesome research fails, horribly killing test subjects, until Arthur finally unites the two parts of the Formula and finds the missing Catalyst—initially hidden inside Claire Bennet, but then transferred into Hiro Nakamura when he time travels. Taking the Catalyst from Hiro, Arthur presents the rapidly transforming Mohinder with his best opportunity to save himself.

THE PRECOG USUTU PAINTS A WARNING ABOUT PINEHEARST. HIS IMAGE SHOWS THE COMPANY'S CORPORATE LOGO WITH FOUR OF ITS VILLAINS—ARTHUR PETRELLI, SYLAR, FLINT GORDON, AND KNOX.

GENISIS

EPISODE 1.1 In the week when a solar eclipse is seen around the world, a group of seemingly unconnected people start to discover special abilities. • Peter Petrelli, a nurse in New York, dreams he can fly. His brother, congressional candidate Nathan Petrelli is dismissive. • Mohinder Suresh, a professor in Madras, India, learns of the death of his father, Chandra, a geneticist. Mohinder travels to Chandra's apartment in Brooklyn, New York, to collect his research papers. • Niki Sanders, a webcam stripper in Las Vegas, is haunted by the reflection of a woman who looks like her. After an assault by debt collectors, Niki regains consciousness to find their dead bodies on her garage floor. • Claire Bennet, a cheerleader from Odessa, Texas, discovers that she can recover instantly from any injury and asks her classmate Zach to film her healings. When Claire rescues a man from a burning train wreck, the incident is reported on TV unknown to Claire. • In Tokyo, Japan, office worker Hiro Nakamura demonstrates to his friend, Ando Masahashi, that he can control time, teleporting himself to Times Square, New York. • Isaac Mendez, a New York artist and junkie, thinks he can paint the future. When his girlfriend, Simone Deveaux, brings nurse Peter to Isaac's apartment after he overdoses, Peter sees a painting of himself flying, and another of an explosion in New York. Convinced he can fly, Peter jumps from a 15-story building. He plummets, is caught by a watching Nathan, who really can fly, but then slips from Nathan's grasp.

DON'T LOOK BACK

EPISODE 1.2 In hospital, Nathan tells Peter his injuries were the result of a fall. Later, Peter's mother, Angela Petrelli, confesses that his father's death was due to suicide. • Mohinder meets Chandra's friend and neighbor, Eden McCain, and they discuss a map on the wall in the apartment. They find a hard drive containing coded information showing that Chandra had discovered a formula for tracing "special" people. • Hiro finds a comic book featuring his own recent adventures. He traces the artist and finds Isaac dead in his apartment, the top of his head removed. The police burst in and arrest him, and as Hiro is questioned by the police, he realises that he seems to have travelled five weeks forward in time. Suddenly there is an explosion and he teleports himself back to Tokyo just in time. • Claire is nearly identified as the train-crash rescuer, but is saved from discovery when another cheerleader, Jackie Wilcox, steps forward and takes the credit. The videotape of Claire's healings goes missing. • After deciding to flee with her son, Micah, Niki finds a new car outside her house and a set of keys with her name on it. In the trunk of the car are the thugs' bodies and a map, which she follows. She arrives in the desert at night to see a spade in the sand. She starts digging and finds a skeleton. • In Los Angeles, a serial killer has murdered a couple and their daughter is missing. Detectives suspect someone called Sylar. Looking over the crime scene, police officer Matt Parkman hears a child's voice in his head and following it, finds the girl, Molly Walker, hidden in the house. • Nathan finds Peter once again at the top of a tall building. Threatening to jump, he forces Nathan to confess that he can fly

ONE GIANT LEAP

EPISODE 1.3 After burying the thugs Niki drives with Micah to her mother-in-law's house. The two women argue about Niki's husband, D.L. Hawkins, who is accused of robbing and murdering "Lindermen's men". As Niki leaves, a police officer stops her and tells her Mr. Linderman wants to see her. • Simone leaves Isaac, frustrated by his drug habit and insistence that he can paint the future. He is plagued by frantic calls from someone calling himself Hiro. • Peter tells Simone, whose dying father Charles he has been nursing, that he is quitting nursing. At an electoral campaign, Nathan tells the audience that Peter's fall was a suicide attempt. Peter storms out followed by Simone. and they begin an affair. • Mohinder and Eden find a notebook with Sylar's address. Breaking into the apartment, they see a copy of Chandra's book, pictures of mutilated corpses, and a map like Chandra's with photos of people pinned to it. • Matt is asked to work with the FBI by detective Audrey Hanson. They foil an attempt by Sylar to abduct Molly, but he regenerates and escapes after being shot. That night, Matt argues with his wife and goes to a bar, where he hears the thoughts of everyone except one man. Leaving, Matt collapses. • At a bonfire party, Brody, a quarterback from school Claire has been flirting with, tries to rape her. In the struggle, she falls and is badly hurt when her head is impaled on a tree branch. She awakens on an autopsy table.• Hiro and Ando fly to Los Angeles, and following the story in the comic book, they rent a car and drive towards Las Vegas.

COLLISION

EPISODE 1.4 Matt briefly regains consciousness to see Claire's father – Mr. Bennet – and the Haitian from the bar standing over him. • Hiro and Ando are down to their last dollar. Hiro uses his powers to cheat at the casino but they are caught and thrown out. • At the hotel, Niki is told that Linderman will cancel her debt if she sexually blackmails Nathan. She hooks up with Nathan but realises she can't go through with the seduction. However, as she starts to leave her alternate personality emerges, a helix symbol visible on her back, and she returns. In the morning, Nathan is dragged from their bed by Mr. Bennet and the Haitian. • Claire's wounds heal and she climbs off the autopsy table and slips away, sneaking into her house. The next day she returns to school, where she confuses a shocked Brody by claiming that his memories were clouded by drunkenness. But after school, she gets back at him by asking if she can drive them both home, and then slamming the car into a wall. • Simone goes to Isaac's apartment to pick up some paintings to sell in her gallery. He refuses to hand over the paintings that show the future. • While preparing to go back to Madras to scatter his father's ashes, Mohinder is approached by Peter, who says he thinks he is one of the people for whom Chandra was searching. He takes Mohinder to see Isaac, but Isaac won't answer the door and they leave. • As Peter and Mohinder travel back on a subway train, time suddenly seems to stand still for everyone but Peter and he sees a Hiro from the future appear, carrying a sword. The Future Hiro says he has a message for Peter.

HIROS

EPISODE 1.5 Future Hiro gives Peter a message which includes the words "Save the cheerleader, save the world," before vanishing. • Nathan escapes from Mr. Bennet by flying away. He lands on a dusty Nevada road, watched by Hiro from a nearby diner. Nathan summons a car to take him back to the hotel, and gives Hiro a lift. • Back at the hotel, Niki warns Nathan about the sex tape. Checking out, he asks the manager about the tape and demands more money from Linderman for his campaign.• At the hospital, Claire tells Mr. Bennet what Brody did, and he gets the Haitian to wipe Brody's mind. • Niki goes home to find police officers looking for D.L., who has escaped custody. • Matt Parkman wakes up on his sofa, having been missing for a day. He begins getting on better with his wife after finding that he can read her thoughts. But later, as he uses his abilities to stop a man robbing a store, the thoughts of other shoppers overwhelm him and he collapses. • Returning to Isaac's loft, Peter sees a painting of a cheerleader and remembers Hiro's message. He arranges the paintings so that they read like a comic strip, and realises that he is able to complete an unfinished painting himself. It shows the cheerleader dead, the top of her head removed. Hiro calls, and Peter says he has a message for him.

BETTER HALVES

EPISODE 1.6 Peter passes on to Hiro the message: "Save the cheerleader, save the world," and tells him he needs to go to New York to find the cheerleader. Peter notices that there is one painting missing in the "comic strip" story, and Isaac says Simone has that one. • Claire's adoptive father, Mr.. Bennet, tells Claire that he has arranged for her to meet her birth parents. However, they are imposters secretly working for him. While listening in on their conversation with Claire, Mr. Bennet gets a call from Eden telling him about Peter and his "Save the cheerleader" message. • Hiro and Ando are stopped by one of the men they cheated at the casino. He takes them to a warehouse poker game to try to win his money back, but they catch sight of a gun, are scared and escape through a bathroom window. • D.L., who has his own special powers, phases into Niki's house. He reassures her of his innocence and tells her he has arranged to see a money launderer to find out who really took Linderman's $2 million. But the next day, when Niki and D.L. arrive at the money launderers, they find the warehouse poker players, dead. • Niki's alternate personality tells her that that it was she who set up D.L.'s crew and stole Linderman's money and that it is hidden in a space above her ceiling. Looking for it, Niki is confronted by D.L. and the alternate personality, Jessica, attacks him. They struggle and D.L. leaves, taking Micah. • As Isaac looks at one of his paintings, he rubs the paint on the back of the figure of a woman and the helix symbol is exposed. At that moment, there's a knock at the door. It's Eden.

NOTHING TO HIDE

EPISODE 1.7 Zach finds Claire's tape and hands it over, but her brother Lyle sneaks a look at it. • Peter finds out that Simone sold the missing painting to Linderman. He asks Nathan to help retrieve it, but Nathan is worried about exposing his association with Linderman. A reporter is asking awkward questions about Linderman and also about a blonde woman, but Peter comes up with a cover story. • Audrey and Matt view the radioactive corpse of murdered oncologist Robert Fresco. A fingerprint leads them to a man named Theodore Sprague whom they trace to a hospital where his wife Karen is dying of cancer. Theodore confesses that he killed Fresco because he couldn't help Karen. His anger is making him emit dangerous levels of radiation, but Matt calms him and he is taken in. Two marks are visible on his neck. • In the locker room at work, Matt's ex-partner, Tom, comes up to talk to him and, reading his thoughts, Matt finds out that Tom has been sleeping with his wife. • Nathan calls Linderman about the missing painting and hears that it's at the gallery. He goes to Peter's apartment, where Peter urges him to tell his wheelchair-bound wife Heidi the truth about Niki. • Micah's technopathic abilities enable him to use a broken payphone to call Niki and tell her where he and D.L. are. Jessica answers, and after hanging up she loads a gun.

HOME COMING

EPISODE 1.9 Claire is preparing for her school's Homecoming Queen celebrations, but Mr. Bennet, worried for her safety, grounds her and sends Eden to the school to find and take out Sylar. Later, he discovers Claire has escaped and follows her to the school. • Nathan receives the missing painting from Mr. Linderman and destroys it, thinking that he is helping Peter. But Simone has made a digital copy, which she shows Peter. It depicts his dead body outside Union Wells High School and a clock showing 8.12 p.m. Peter leaves for Union Wells. • In the Nevada desert, Jessica buys a rifle, telling the seller that she is going after somebody who took her son. Meanwhile D.L. tries to comfort a confused Micah who can't understand why Niki is no longer with them. • Mohinder dreams of the mysterious boy again, who tells him that he has "the answer". Mohinder wakes in his office, goes to the computer and immediately guesses the password "Shanti". A list of people and locations appears. He decides to return to New York and continue his father's mission. • At the High School, Sylar sees a clipping of the train rescue and thinks Jackie is the girl he is looking for. He kills her, but injures Claire in the process. When he sees Claire's crushed limbs heal, Sylar turns his attention to her. She runs into the bleachers while Peter and Sylar fight, the clock reading 8.12. When Claire comes back she sees the dead Peter regenerate. • Sylar escapes, climbing a hill, but at the top he is met by Eden and the Haitian.

SEVEN MINUTES TO MIDNIGHT

EPISODE 1.8 Back in India, Mohinder finds out that he had an older sister, Shanti, who died when he was two and whom Chandra thought was "special". • Hiro and Ando meet Charlie, a waitress in a Texas diner who can remember everything she reads. She is later found dead, her head ripped open. • Matt discovers that he too has marks on his neck, and that like him, Ted suffers from headaches, saw the Haitian, and blacked out for two days. • Mr. Bennet meets Eden at the Primatech warehouse. Learning that Isaac can only paint the future while high, Mr. Bennet forces her to use her powers to make him shoot up, even though he is trying to quit. Isaac paints an exploding man. • Mohinder sees an Indian boy he recognises from a dream. Chasing him, he is transported to New York and sees Chandra's murder. The boy gives him a key. Waking up, he uses the key to open the desk and finds a file marked "Sanjog, Iyer", and a picture of the boy. • Matt's wife, Janice, admits to the affair with Tom but says it's over. Audrey calls Matt; Ted has escaped. • Hiro goes back in time to try to save Charlie, leaving Ando alone.

SIX MONTHS AGO

EPISODE 1.10 This episode shows what occurred six months before the Heroes timeline. • Hiro teleports to the diner on the wrong day, and is unable to save Charlie. • Eden is using her powers of persuasion to get away with a criminal lifestyle. • Mr. Bennet visits Chandra's apartment to find out how Claire's powers will affect her, but gets no answer. Later, he notices how quickly an injury to her hand heals. • Niki's estranged father, Hal, tries to get back into Niki and Micah's life, but Jessica emerges for the first time and attacks him, accusing him of beating up and killing her. • Nathan tells Peter that the District Attorney wants him to prosecute Mr. Linderman, but he is their father's biggest client and Peter doesn't want their father dragged in to any trouble. Driving home, Nathan survives a car crash unscathed but Heidi is seriously injured. Nathan tells Peter that the accident was caused by Linderman's men. Later, Peter hears that his father is dead, apparently of a heart attack. • While at Chandra Suresh's apartment for tests, clock repairer Gabriel Gray steals the address of suspected telekinetic, Brian Davis. He lures Davis to his shop, introducing himself as Sylar (the name on a watch he is repairing). Sylar kills Brian and acquires his powers. Returning to Chandra's apartment, he demonstrates his ability and offers to help Chandra find the other special people.

GODSEND

EPISODE 1.12 Hiro steals a sword belonging to the legendary Japanse hero Takezo Kensei from a museum, hoping it will restore his powers, but it is a replica. • Linderman's associate, Aron Malski, tells D.L. that Niki has confessed and charges against him have been dropped, and D.L. hands over the money. • An FBI agent questions Mohinder about a woman named Sarah Ellis. Shown a picture, he recognizes Eden. He is told that she has committed suicide. • D.L. and Micah visit Niki in jail. Niki turns violent when she is isn't allowed to hug Micah and is put into a straightjacket, but hears Jessica promising to free her. • Nathan is angry that Simone showed Peter the painting. They find Isaac back in his apartment. Later, Hiro and Ando arrive. • After two weeks in a coma, Peter slips away from the hospital. He sees a bearded man stealing a wallet and realizes he is invisible to everyone else. He challenges him and Peter too becomes invisible. • Simone tells Hiro that Mr. Linderman buys all Isaac's paintings. She offers to arrange a meeting between Mr. Linderman and Hiro.

THE FIX

EPISODE 1.13 Peter asks Claude Rains, the invisible man, to help him control his powers but he refuses. • Micah uses his powers to draw money from an ATM for D.L. • Hiro and Ando are bundled into a car by strange men and driven to a secluded building. There, they meet the "big boss," who turns out to be Hiro's father Kaito Nakamura. • Nathan begs Mohinder to find a way to "fix" Peter. They go to Peter's apartment to talk to him, but he runs out, straight into Claude. Claude now agrees to try to help Peter control his powers. • Claire learns from the Haitain that her real mother died in an explosion 14 years ago. She finds an old newspaper story about a woman and baby dying in a fire. Claire traces the woman's relatives and ends up speaking to the supposedly dead women, Meredith Gordon. Claire realizes that she is the baby everyone thought was dead. • Matt is suspended for six months, but cheers up when he learns that Janice is pregnant. • Hank, guarding the captive Sylar, believes his prisoner has died and takes off his restraints. When Mr. Bennet arrives he finds Sylar very much alive, and Hank murdered.

DISTRACTIONS

EPISODE 1.14 Aron Malsky tells Niki that the charges against her have been dropped. She is free to go home, but Jessica now seems to have taken permanent control of Niki. • Sylar locks Mr. Bennet inside the cell and leaves, taking his driving licence. He goes to the Bennets' house and questions Mrs Bennet about Claire, but while he waits for her to come home a freed Mr. Bennet arrives with the Haitian. Sylar flees. • Hiro's father, Kaito, orders him to return to Yamagato Industries and accept an Executive-Vice-President role. When Hiro refuses, his father reacts with anger and tears up the painting of Hiro and the dinosaur, but Hiro cleverly makes his father realize that his sister Kimiko, not he, is the ideal candidate for the job. • After a secret visit from Claire to her trailer park home, Meredith contacts Claire's real father, Nathan Petrelli, who offers money. • On the rooftop of the Deveaux building, Simone and Isaac talk, watched by an invisible Peter and Claude. Challenging Peter to fly, Claude pushes him off the roof. He plummets 30 stories, smashes into a taxi, regenerates, and begins to rapidly manifest all kinds of powers at once. Claude saves him by knocking him out. • Isaac paints a picture of Peter by the cab, partially visible. He tells Mr. Bennet that Peter might be invisible, and Mr. Bennet realizes that Claude might not be dead, as he believed.

FALLOUT

EPISODE 1.11 Peter is in custody, suspected of being Sylar and murdering Jackie the cheerleader. Meanwhile, the real Sylar, seriously injured, is being held by Mr. Bennet and Eden in a secure room at Primatech. • In Utah, D.L. and Micah run from Jessica. They take refuge in a forest cabin, but Jessica finds them after Micah contacts her, thinking he is communicating with Niki. Jessica attacks D.L., injuring Micah in the process. Niki returns, and, frightened by what she is capable of, confesses to murder to a highway patrolman. • Claire tells Mr. Bennet that Lyle and Zach know about her powers, and later finds they both seem to have had their minds wiped. • Audrey and Matt question Claire and Mr. Bennet, but Matt finds he is unable to read their thoughts because of static, which he doesn't realize is being created by the Haitian. • Hiro and Ando arrive in Texas too late to "save the cheerleader," but then get a call from Isaac asking to meet them. He has been given a cell phone and freed by Eden. Isaac tells Hiro and Ando about his picture of the exploding man. They encourage him to try another painting, and thus time he produces a picture of Hiro with a sword, and a Tyrannosaurus Rex. • Eden goes to Sylar's cell and suggests to him that he should blast his brains out with her gun, but he uses his powers of telekinesis to make her shoot herself in the head instead. • Peter collapses as Nathan collects him from jail. Awakening, remembers a dream in which he saw himself exploding. He tells Nathan he is the cause of the explosion before lapsing into unconsciousness again.

RUN!

EPISODE 1.15 Nathan visits Meredith in her trailer, offering her money on condition she doesn't tell the world about Claire. He believes this would harm his electoral campaign. He has narrowly missed Claire herself, who left the trailer shortly before, and she returns to listen outside. As Nathan drives away, Claire hurls a rock at his car. She returns home to find her mother no longer seems to recognise her or her beloved pet dog, Mr. Muggles. • Jessica has managed to convince D.L. and Micah that she is Niki. When she is alone, she opens a package that has arrived for her. It contains a photograph of someone Linderman wants her to kill. It's Aron Malsky. • Having been suspended from the LAPD, Matt takes a position with a private security firm. His first job is escorting Malsky to a meeting about diamonds, but by thought-reading, Matt realizes that it's a set-up. As Matt tries to rush Malsky from the building, hit-woman Jessica hunts them down and eventually catches up with them. Matt survives, but is unable to save Malsky. His story is met with scepticism from the police, and he decides not to hand over Malsky's diamonds. • Hiro and Ando go back to the hotel, looking for the real Kensei sword, held by Linderman. A woman called Hope cons the "two Chinese guys" into helping her cheat her partner. When she realises Hiro is on to her scheme, she locks him in a closet and leaves with Ando and a suitcase. • Sylar murders Zane Taylor, one of the people on Chandra's list, and steals his ability: turning things to liquid. Posing as Zane, he offers to help Mohinder trace everyone else with abilities. • Jessica receives another package with another picture of a target. This time it's Nathan.

UNEXPECTED

EPISODE 1.16 Isaac warns Mr. Bennet that Peter will destroy New York. One of the paintings shows the roof of the Deveaux building, and thinking that Peter might return there, Mr. Bennet gives Isaac a gun. • In Montana, Mohinder and Sylar introduce themselves to Dale Smither, a woman on Chandra's list who possesses super-powerful hearing. Later, Sylar goes back to her house alone and murders Dale, stealing her power. • Steve Gustavson, the Gaming Commission Officer who is also Hope's partner, frees Hiro from the closet and they go after Hope and Ando. When they catch up with them there is a gunfight, and Hiro uses his powers to save Ando from a fatal shot. Feeling guilty about getting his friend into danger, he jumps on a bus alone to continue his mission. • On top of the Deveaux building, Claude and Peter narrowly escape being shot by Mr. Bennet and the Haitian who are watching them through thermal vision goggles. Claude blames Peter, for leading "them" straight to him, and abandons him. • Mrs Bennet has been diagnosed with a brain haemorrhage, but seems to be recovering. • Ted and Matt meet Hana Gitelman, who is able to send and receive wireless signals. She tells them the marks on their necks were made by a needle that injects a radioactive isotope for tracking viruses. A shipment of the needles apparently went to Primatech Paper Co. • Peter goes to see Isaac, blaming him for Claude's departure, and they fight. Isaac fires the gun at what he thinks is the invisible Peter but the shot kills Simone, who has just let herself in.

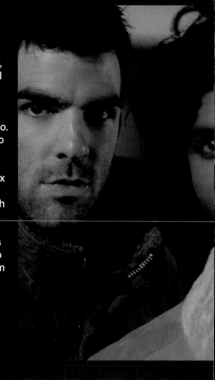

COMPANY MAN

EPISODE 1.17 Ted and Matt break into the Bennet home. They confront Mr. Bennet, and Matt reads Claire's thoughts about Mr. Bennet wiping minds and about her healing abilites. • In flashbacks, Thompson of the Company gives Mr. Bennet a cover as a Primatech manager and introduces him to his partner, Claude; Kaito Nakamura hands baby Claire to Mr. Bennet but says he must return her if any abilities manifest; Mr. Bennet learns about a Haitian who can wipe memories; and Mr. Bennet seemingly kills Claude when he questions the ethics of the Company. • Back in the present, Matt and Mr. Bennet are unable to pacify Ted. He ties up Lyle and Mrs Bennet, then sends Matt and Mr. Bennet to Primatech for information. • Mr. Bennet and Matt return with a tranquilizer to knock Ted out. But before they can use it, Thompson appears and shoots Ted, setting off his powers and causing explosions. Claire enters the fire to tranquilize Ted. She emerges badly burned and Thompson watches as she heals. • Thompson holds Ted and Matt captive. He asks Mr. Bennet to bring Claire in but instead he picks her up and drives to a bridge, where the Haitian is waiting. He has him shoot and injure him, and wipe his mind, so that the Company can't trace Claire through him.

PARASITE

EPISODE 1.18 As Mr. Bennet agonises over a missing Claire, his wife whispers that she is safe. • Claire evades the Haitian and goes to Peter's apartment, where she meets Angela. • Mohinder realizes "Zane" is really Sylar. He drugs him, takes samples of his spinal fluid, and shoots him, but Sylar stops the bullet. • Hiro steals the Kensei sword helped by Ando, who has been following him. They escape by teleportation, but arrive in a future New York after the explosion. • At the police quiz Isaac about Simone, she suddenly walks in. But after they leave, she transforms into another woman. Mr. Bennet, appears and introduces her as Candice. Later, Isaac shoots up and starts painting again. • Arriving at the Corinthian hotel for a meeting, Nathan discovers that Linderman knows he is working for the FBI. He resolves to kill him, but changes his mind when Linderman reveals that he knows about Nathan and Peter, and predicts that Nathan will be president one day. • Impersonating Mrs Bennet, Candice gets Mr. Bennet to confirm what he knows about Claire, then summons Thompson. • Peter finds Mohinder fixed to the ceiling of his aparment, dripping blood, and is then himself attacked by Sylar.

.07%

EPISODE 1.19 Mr. Bennet, Matt, and Ted combine their powers and escape from their cells at Primatech. At the Burnt Toast Diner, they discuss going to New York. • Linderman tries to convince Nathan the explosion will be a catalyst for healing the world, and that only 0.07% of the world's population will die. • After a struggle Sylar kills Peter with a shard of glass, but Mohinder gets free and knocks him out. When Sylar awakens, Peter, Mohinder and the list are gone, but he finds a piece of comic with Isaac's address. • At Angela's house Nathan, Angela and Mohinder are grieving over Peter's body when Claire pulls out the shard and Peter regenerates. Later, Nathan tells Claire to go to Paris with Angela, where they will both be safe from the coming explosion. • D.L. is leaving Jessica, tired of her violent ways. When she arrives to say goodby to Micah, she finds he has already been taken by a Niki imposter: Candice. • Sylar kills Isaac in his apartment, but not before Isaac tells him he has a way of explaining to the others how to defeat Sylar. • In the future, in a devastated New York, Hiro and Ando search Isaac's apartment. They find a map made of notes and clippings and are met by a Future Hiro.

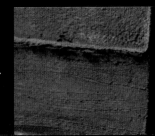

FIVE YEARS GONE

EPISODE 1.20 A security team including Matt and the Haitian bursts into the apartment and captures Hiro as a suspected terrorist, but Future Hiro and Ando escape. • They are in a strange world five years after the explosion, where people with special abilities are seen as a threat and are arrested as terrorists. Nathan is President, and Mohinder his advisor. • Mr. Bennet, still at Primatech, is secretly helping special people to conceal their powers and avoid arrest. Matt, now the brutal head of Homeland Security, turns a blind eye to this in return for protection for his own family. With D.L. and Micah seemingly dead, Niki is now Peter's girlfriend. Claire is a waitress living under a false identity and looking forward to getting married. • Realizing the Hiro he has captured is not the Future Hiro he has been hunting, Matt falls out with Mr. Bennet about whether to tell the President. Matt shoots Mr. Bennet and turns Claire over to the President. But it becomes clear that Nathan isn't Nathan at all, but Sylar, who attacks Claire and slices open her head. • Hiro escapes when Mohinder, given the task of executing him, can't go through with it and kills the Haitian instead. • Peter finds out that the real Nathan was killed by Sylar and as the two men fight, Hiro takes the opportunity to teleport back to his own time with Ando, leaving Future Hiro to the mercy of Matt.

THE HARD PART

EPISODE 1.21 Hiro and Ando follow Sylar to his mother's house. She becomes agitated when Sylar demonstrates his powers, and attacks Sylar with a pair of scissors. As he struggles to calm her, he accidentally stabs and kills her. Hiro cannot stop time for long enough to kill Sylar, and he and Ando quickly teleport back to Isaac's apartment where they notice Hiro's sword is broken. • Mr. Bennet, Matt, and Ted begin the drive to New York to bring down the Walker Tracking System. • D.L. and Jessica discover that the woman who picked up Micah was working for Linderman, and that Linderman has gone to New York. Meanwhile, Micah catches on that Candice is not really Niki, but when he tries to escape she throws strange illusions around him and threatens to make things even worse. • Mohinder joins forces with the Company to try to stop Sylar. Thompson introduces him to Molly Walker, who has a virus that only one other person—Mohinder's sister Shanti—has had. Molly has the ability to locate and stop Sylar, but the virus is blocking her powers. Mohinder realizes that antibodies in his own blood are the cure. • Peter wants Claire to remain in New York to help stop the explosion. Nathan is having doubts about going along with Linderman's plan, but Angela strongly urges him to go ahead. • Later, Peter hands Claire a gun and tells her she must shoot him in the back of the head if he becomes dangerous as that is the one injury he won't be able to regenerate from. As they leave the Petrelli mansion, they unexpectedly meet Mr. Bennet, Matt, and Ted, and Ted's powers are immediately absorbed by Peter.

LANDSLIDE

EPISODE 1.22 Hiro's father reappears and says it is time for him to instruct Hiro in the art of the swordsman. As Hiro receives his training, Ando buys a sword and goes after Sylar. • Peter tells Ted that either of them could cause the explosion and that they must leave New York, and Sylar uses his super hearing to listen. Calling himself Isaac Mendez, he summons the FBI who seize Ted, but Peter and Claire escape. • Linderman tries to secure Nathan's loyalty by restoring Heidi's ability to walk. • On polling day, Candice gets Micah to influence the machines so Nathan wins by a landslide. • Nathan is persuaded to reveal Linderman's location to D.L. and Jessica, who join Matt and Mr. Bennet as they close in on the tracking system. Between them they breach the Kirby Plaza Building, and Matt and Mr. Bennet take out Thompson and find the system—it's Molly, cured of her virus. • D.L. and Jessica find Linderman, but when he offers her money to kill D.L. she refuses, and Niki instantly returns. D.L. phases his fist into Linderman's brain and kills him, but takes a non-fatal bullet. • Sylar intercepts a police van carrying Ted and kills him, taking his powers. Now, either he or Peter could be the cause of the explosion.

HOW TO STOP AN EXPLODING MAN

EPISODE 1.23 Against Claire's wishes, Peter tells Nathan about Sylar, but reading his thoughts realizes it was a mistake. Meanwhile, Claire runs away straight into Angela's arms. • Molly locates Sylar, but when Mr. Bennet calls Claire to tell her and Peter where to find him, she is with Angela. Matt says he himself will stop Sylar, and leaves for Isaac's loft. Later, Claire escapes from Nathan and Angela by jumping out of the window, instantly healing from her injuries. • In Isaac's loft, Hiro saves Ando from Sylar by teleporting him back to Japan. He tells Ando his involvement is at an end. • Niki climbs the stairs of the Kirby Plaza Building and finds Jessica, who taunts her with an unconscious and bleeding Micah. The two women fight, and Niki realizes that this isn't Jessica at all but Candice. When Niki punches Candice, she and the illusion of Micah disappear and the real Micah is heard shouting for help from a closet. • Peter is awakened from a strange dream by Mr. Bennet, Molly having tracked him down. They go to Kirby Plaza, and Sylar attacks Peter just as Niki ,Micah, D.L., Mohinder, and Molly emerge from the Kirby Plaza building. None of their efforts succeed in stopping Sylar, and Peter begins glowing. Claire is about to take the last resort of shooting him when Nathan appears, lifts Peter up and flies away with him. Hiro stabs Sylar, and the others watch as an explosion lights up the sky.

FOUR MONTHS LATER...

EPISODE 2.1 It is now four months since the explosion high above New York. • After trying to warn the world about a disease that will wipe out evolved humans, Mohinder is contacted by a Company member named Bob and invited to join the Company. This was Mohinder's aim: he plans to work with Mr. Bennet to bring down the Company from within. • Claire and her family have moved to California, taking the name of Butler. At her new school, Claire attracts the interest of classmate West Rosen, who is concealing his own powers of flight. • Hiro is teleported into the middle of a battle in seventeenth century Japan. He meets his hero Takezo Kensei, but is disappointed to learn that Kensei is really a not very heroic Englishman. • Matt, now an NYPD detective, is divorced from Janice and looking after Molly. She has been suffering from nightmares about somebody watching her. • Nathan is depressed and has taken to drinking. He has fallen out with Angela, blaming her for Peter's death. • Brother and sister Alejandro and Maya Herrera try to escape Honduras, where they are wanted for homicide. Maya has a strange ability to kill. When it manifests, her eyes fill with dark fluid and so do the eyes of her victims. Only the presence of Alejandro seems to enable her to control her power. • Kaito Nakamura and Angela Petrelli each find a photograph of themselves marked with a helix, and believe they are about to die. Shortly afterwards, Kaito is murdered on the rooftop of the Deveaux building. • In a shipyard in Cork, Ireland, thieves break into a cargo container and find an amnesiac Peter, wearing a helix necklace.

EPISODE 2.2 Mr. Bennet (Noah) shows Sandra a painting depicting Kaito's murder. It is one of a series of eight Isaac completed before he died, but Noah doesn't know where the other seven are. • Hiro stands in for a drunk Kensei to rescue a swordsmith's daughter from bandits. He then persuades Kensei to come and rescue the swordsmith, but as they set out, Kensei is killed. However, he spontaneously regenerates. • Ricky, the leader of the thieves, hears that Peter beat up the son of the criminal he works for to save Caitlin, his sister, from assault. He says if Peter will help with a robbery he will hand over a box he found with Peter in the cargo container that might hold clues about his past. • Bob sends Mohinder to cure the Haitian of the virus. Unknown to Bob, Mohinder reunites the Haitian and Noah. • During their escape from Honduras, Alejandro and Maya become separated and Maya's powers nearly kill her friend, Nidia. Alejandro catches up with her just in time. • Matt is investigating Kaito's murder. He learns from Ando that the helix symbol is linked to Takezo Kensei and means "godsend". When he questions Angela, she realizes he is reading her mind, but is unable to resist. She is later attacked by an unknown assailant. • Molly is still drawing the helix and eyes watching her. • At school, Claire asks questions about lizard regeneration in biology class, and West suggests she read Chandra's book. Later, he secretly watches as she experimentally chops off her toe and sees it regenerate.

KINDRED

EPISODE 2.3 Niki goes to ask the Company if they can cure her, leaving Micah with his great aunt, Nana Dawson, in New Orleans. • Sylar is being nursed by Candice, now calling herself Michelle. Having lost his powers, he kills her and tries to steal hers but fails. • Ando finds scrolls inside the Kensei sword, with messages from Hiro. Hiro is in love with Yaeko, the swordsmith's daughter, but she is to marry Kensei. Hiro forces Kensei to become a hero, then tries to return to his own time but can't. • West tells Claire about his powers and she thinks her father is involved. • When Alejandro is arrested Maya kills everyone in the police station except him. Freed, he revives the victims and he and Maya leave with Derek, another prisoner. • After a robbery, Peter uses his powers to save Ricky when his brother Will pulls a gun on him. He gets his box and Caitlin tattoos him with the family tattoo, but it changes into the helix. • The Company gives Mohinder a new laboratory in Isaac's old loft. There he finds the eighth painting from Isaac's final series. It shows Noah dead, a bullet hole in his glasses.

THE KINDNESS OF STRANGERS

EPISODE 2.4 Claire begins dating West, concealing the affair from her father. • Angela confesses to killing Kaito, but Matt knows she is lying to protect somebody. Nathan produces the group photo from which the helix photos of Kaito and Angela were taken. It shows Mr. and Mrs Petrelli, Bob, Charles Deveaux, Kaito, Matt's father Maury, and five other people. They speculate that the people in the photo are being picked off one by one. • Driving to the border, Alejandro, Maya, and Derek pick up the injured Sylar, who quickly realizes that Alejandro and Maya have powers. After murdering a suspicious Derek, Sylar offers to help them to get to New York. • Micah impresses his cousin Damon by making his television transmit a wrestling match although they had not paid to view it. The next day, Micah's other cousin, Monica, stops a robbery at the burger restaurant where she works by copying a move she saw in the wrestling match. • Noah and the Haitian plan a trip to Odessa, Ukraine, to look for Isaac's missing final paintings. • Matt wants Molly to find his father, but when he shows her the photograph of Maury she screams because he is the man in her nightmares. She successfully locates Maury, but the shock renders her unconscious. As he holds Molly in his arms, Matt reads her mind and hears her screaming for help.

FIGHT OR FLIGHT

EPISODE 2.5 Micah realizes Monica is a "copycat"—she can mimic the actions of others. • Matt and Nathan trace Maury, but he throws confusing illusions around them and escapes. Later, they find a photo of Bob marked with the helix death threat. • Against Noah's advice, Mohinder takes Molly to the Company for help. While there, Bob asks him to find a girl (Monica Dawson), when Niki bursts in. She attacks Bob but is restrained. Mohinder leaves to find Monica. • Ando, back in Tokyo, reads messages from Hiro via the series of scrolls. He reads how Hiro, Kensei, and Yaeko have reached the camp of a villain called White Beard who is holding Yaeko's father. • Peter opens the box but nothing sparks his memory. He and Caitlin are now a couple. A woman named Elle is looking for Peter, and uses her electrical powers to kill Ricky when he won't reveal his whereabouts.

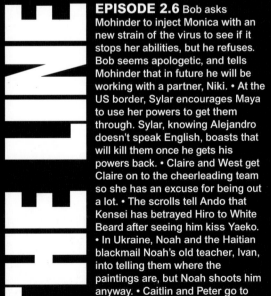

THE LINE

EPISODE 2.6 Bob asks Mohinder to inject Monica with an new strain of the virus to see if it stops her abilities, but he refuses. Bob seems apologetic, and tells Mohinder that in future he will be working with a partner, Niki. • At the US border, Sylar encourages Maya to use her powers to get them through. Sylar, knowing Alejandro doesn't speak English, boasts that will kill them once he gets his powers back. • Claire and West get Claire on to the cheerleading team so she has an excuse for being out a lot. • The scrolls tell Ando that Kensei has betrayed Hiro to White Beard after seeing him kiss Yaeko. • In Ukraine, Noah and the Haitian blackmail Noah's old teacher, Ivan, into telling them where the paintings are, but Noah shoots him anyway. • Caitlin and Peter go to Montreal, but they are teleported to New York, one year in the future, and the city has been evacuated.

OUT OF TIME

EPISODE 2.7 Noah destroys Isaac's paintings after taking pictures to show Mohinder. • In the future New York, Peter and Caitlin are quarantined and learn that the virus has wiped out 93% of the world's population. Angela comes to see Peter, and his memories begin to return, but while trying to rescue Caitlin he is teleported back to Montreal. • Hiro fails to persuade Kensei to fight on the side of good, and uses his powers to escape back to his own time. • West recognises Noah as the man who abducted him, and thinking Claire has plotted to trap him, he flies off. • Bob tells Nathan the person trying to kill the Company founders is Adam Monroe, but he is using Maury to do it. Matt enters Maury's nightmare in which he is holding Molly captive, and realizing that he has similar powers to his father, he shatters the illusion and saves Molly. • Niki injects herself with the virus when Maury messes with her mind. Mohinder's blood no longer works as an antidote, and Bob proposes that Claire's abilities might be able to cure it. • Noah is worried Claire is about to be exposed and demands they pack up and leave Costa Verde. • In Montreal, Peter is trying to get back to New York and Caitlin when he is confronted by Adam Monroe, who is the same person as Takezo Kensei.

FOUR MONTHS AGO...

EPISODE 2.8 These are the events that happened in the four months after the explosion. • Nathan escapes death but suffers terrible radiation burns. Peter is captured by Bob and Elle of the Company, who promise to cure him of his unwanted powers. • At Alejandro's wedding, Maya sees the bride cheating on her husband with an old flame. Her power manifests for the first time, and she kills everyone except herself and Alejandro. She flees and takes refuge in a convent. When Alejandro finds her, the two of them go on the run from the police. • Niki stops taking the medication provided by the Company to control her split personality, because the side effects are dulled emotions. As they wear off, a new persona, Gina, emerges. D.L. follows Gina to a night club in Los Angeles. To get her back, he assaults a clubber who shoots him dead. • While being treated by the Company, Peter meets Adam in an adjoining cell. Adam convinces him not to trust the Company and they escape. They find Nathan in hospital and cure his burns using Adam's blood, but they are hunted down by Elle and the Haitian. The Haitian is under orders to capture Peter but instead wipes his memory and locks him in a storage crate. • Back in present-day Montreal, prompted by Adam, Peter's memories come flooding back.

CAUTIONARY TALES

EPISODE 2.9 Claire refuses to flee from Costa Verde with the Bennet family. Noah asks West to convince her that it is for the best, and explains that Claire hadn't betrayed him. • Bob wants Mohinder to work with his daughter, Elle, to find Claire and "take out" Noah. Mohinder refuses to kill anyone and threatens to expose the Company, so Bob agrees to capture Noah alive instead. But the attempt to get Claire goes wrong and ends with Noah and West taking Elle hostage. • Returning home, Noah finds Claire has been kidnapped by Bob. In retaliation, he ties Elle to a chair with her feet in a doggy bath so she cannot use her powers without hurting herself. Noah then calls Bob to suggest they exchange hostages, and after taking some blood from Claire, Bob agrees. • The exchange is ruined when Elle, freed, shocks West and Claire, so they fall to the ground. Noah reacts by shooting Elle in the arm. Then, to prevent Noah from killing Bob, Mohinder shoots him in the eye, creating the scene shown in Isaac's painting. Later, at the Company facility, Noah is revived with a transfusion of Claire's blood. • Hiro time travels, in an attempt to prevent his father's death. Although Kaito forbids this, Hiro is able to witness the murder and identify his father's assassin—Takezo Kensei, or Adam Monroe. • Matt uses his new mind-controlling abilities to get Angela to reveal the names of Kaito's killer and the unidentified woman in the photograph of the Company founders. They are Adam Monroe and Victoria Pratt.

TRUTH & CONSEQUENCES

EPISODE 2.10 Claire's blood has not only revived Noah but reactivated the virus antibodies in Mohinder's blood. Mohinder tells Bob to destroy all the strains of the virus, and calls Niki to say he has found a cure for her. • Reunited with Niki, Micah wants to show her D.L.'s bravery medal but it has been taken by Damon. When Monica tries to retrieve it, the gang who have it kidnap her. • Sylar is finding it easy to control Maya. He teaches her to control her powers and he kills Alejandro. • Peter and Adam find Victoria Pratt, the biological engineer who discovered the Shanti Virus and Adam shoots her, but not before Peter reads her mind to discover that 138, the most lethal strain, is in Odessa, Texas. • As Claire scatters Noah's ashes, given to her by Bob, she confronts Elle, threatening to go public with her powers. • Arriving in New York, Sylar calls Mohinder, who is on his way to New Orleans. He demands that Mohinder see Maya, threatening Molly if he is refused. • From Kaito's files, Hiro identifies Kensei as Adam Monroe. He locates him at Primatech where he and Peter are looking for the Shanti virus.

POWERLESS

EPISODE 2.11 Nathan and Matt tell Angela that Peter is alive and working with Adam. She urges them to go to Primatech and stop Adam from releasing the lethal virus. They arrive at Primatech to find Peter has knocked out Hiro, but manage to persuade him of Adam's evil intentions, and using telekinesis, Peter seizes the virus and turns it to dust. • Hiro avenges Kaito's murder by trapping Adam in a casket in a Japanese cemetery. • Niki and Micah try to save Monica from a burning warehouse where she has been tied up by the gang. Monica and Micah escape, but the building explodes while Niki is still inside. • Claire is about to expose the Company's activities when Noah reappears. He tells her that he has made a deal with the Company and they will leave their family alone. • When Maya finally realizes Sylar is evil and killed Alejandro, he shoots her. He asks Mohinder to inject her with Claire's blood, planning to use it on himself if it works. It does, but at that moment Elle bursts in, having seen Sylar on a surveillance camera, and Sylar runs away, taking the blood. • Nathan calls a press conference, planning to come clean about the Company and the evolved humans, but as it begins he is shot in the chest. Watching a report about the assassination on TV, Angela makes an ominous phone call to an unknown person.

THE SECOND COMING

EPISODE 3.1 Four years in the future, Peter, a scar across his face, escapes from a gun-toting Claire back to the present day. He shoots Nathan at his press conference, then seemingly escapes as Present-day Peter and Matt Parkman chase him. • Peter revives the dead Nathan a kiss. After his miraculous recovery Nathan finds religion. • After discovering that Peter is really Future Peter, Matt is suddenly transported to the desert in Africa, where he sees a rock painting of the world exploding. • In hospital, Nathan gets a visit from Linderman. The governor of New York sees Nathan's story on TV, and discusses it with a woman called Tracy Strauss who looks like Niki. • Future Peter tells Angela Petrelli that he has put Present-day Peter somewhere safe. • Sylar captures Claire, opens her skull, and absorbs her power. As she begins to heal he leaves, taking Noah's list of "villains." • At the Company, on Level 5 an imprisoned man screams that he is Peter Petrelli. • Disobeying a DVD warning from Kaito, Hiro opens a safe and finds half of a molecular Formula inside, but it is immediately stolen by a "speedster" named Daphne. Traveling to the future to see what will happen, Hiro sees Ando killing him and explosions rocking the world. • Mohinder discovers that the adrenal glands are the source of special powers. He develops a formula to give powers to anyone and injects himself. He collapses, but when thieves try to rob him he finds that he now has super-strength and fights them off. Behind him is a painting of the world exploding.

THE BUTTERFLY EFFECT

EPISODE 3.2 Mohinder notices he is growing scales. • In the African desert, Matt meets Usutu, the man who painted the rock picture of the future. • Hiro and Ando follow Daphne to a Paris apartment full of stolen objects, and Hiro manages to plant a tracking device on her. • When Tracy visits Nathan to offer him a seat on the Senate, he thinks she is Niki Sanders. Later, he realizes that he is the only person who can see Linderman. • Claire is now unable to feel pain, and is worried she is becoming less human. • Finding Bob with his brain cut out, Elle realizes Sylar is nearby. She releases Noah, who shoots Sylar, but he heals and attacks Elle. She emits an electrical charge that stuns him, and allows all the prisoners to escape. Later, Angela, now head of the Company, fires Elle. • Future Peter reveals himself to Nathan. • As Tracy takes Nathan's acceptance call, she is approached by a reporter who has the Niki sex tape. In anger she puts her hand on his arm, and he turns to ice and shatters. • Noah leaves Claire in the care of her natural mother Meredith while he goes to hunt the villains. • Future Peter has left Present-day Peter in the body of one of the escapees, Jesse Murphy. Now, not wanting to reveal himself, Peter must watch as the other villains commit acts of violence. • Angela reveals to Sylar that she is his mother.

EPISODE 3.3 Angela is now "feeding" Sylar with victims. • Tracy finds out that Niki has died, but with Micah's help discovers that she and Niki were born on the same day, at the same hospital, and were both delivered by Dr. Zimmerman. She tracks down the doctor. • Present-day Peter, in Jesse's body, is traveling with the escapees Flint, Knox, and the German when they embark on a bank robbery in which the German dies. • Angela sends Noah and Sylar after the robbers. During the fight, Future Peter whisks Present-day Peter away and Jesse returns. Saved by Sylar, Noah arrests Flint and asks Sylar to bring in Jesse and Knox, but Sylar cannot resist the urge to kill Jesse, and lets Knox escape. • Hiro and Ando follow Daphne to Berlin, Germany. They manage to get the other half of the Formula from the Haitian, but this half too is stolen by Daphne. Hiro and Ando are arrested by the Company. • Claire asks Meredith to teach her to fight. Later, she finds Noah's files with details of people with powers. • Usutu reveals other paintings of Matt's future. He obliterates a happy scene of Matt with a new family, covering it with a painting of Matt grieving a dead woman. He offers Matt some paste to eat. Matt eats it, his eyes turn white and he begins to see the future.

EPISODE 3.4 Dr. Zimmerman tells Tracy that she was one of triplets: Tracy, Niki, and Barbara. DNA experiments on the triplets gave them powers. Horrified, Tracy attempts suicide but Nathan saves her. They reveal their powers to each other and begin an affair. • Future Peter takes Present-day Peter four years forward in time, where the Formula has become freely available with dangerous results. When Future Claire shoots Future Peter, Present-day Peter escapes to look for help from Sylar. • Peter learns Sylar's new address from Future Mohinder, whose mutation is now advanced. Peter finds Future Sylar living an ordinary life in Costa Verde as Gabriel Gray, and raising a young son, named Noah. Sylar reveals to Peter that they are brothers. He agrees to give Peter his power, but warns him that he will now have the "hunger." • Daphne, Matt's wife in this future timeline, uses Molly to pinpoint Peter at Sylar's house. She goes there with Claire and Knox intending to kill Peter, but Sylar's son is accidentally killed instead. Gabriel's anger makes him lose control of his powers, and he explodes, devastating Costa Verde and killing 200,000 people. • In this future timeline, Nathan is President and he and Tracy are married. He tries to talk to Peter, but Peter now has Sylar's "hunger" and only just restrains himself from killing Nathan. • Back in the present, Peter challenges Sylar in his cell. • Matt wakes from a dream about Daphne returning home seriously hurt and dying in his arms. Usutu shows him his spirit guide—a tortoise. • After a hint from Angela, Hiro and Ando go to Japan to release Adam Monroe from his grave.

ANGELS AND MONSTERS

EPISODE 3.5 Mohinder is trapping people in cocoons in his lab. • Sylar stops Peter from opening Angela's skull, then goes on another job with Noel. • Claire tries to help a misunderstood villain, Stephen Canfield, but when Noah and Sylar burst in he escapes via a vortex. Sylar saves Claire from being dragged in. • In Japan, Knox abducts Adam. Knox and Daphne invite Hiro to join the Pinehearst Company, but first he must pass a test by killing Ando. He appears to stab Ando with a sword. • Nathan and Tracy visit Angela. She says that the Company gave them their powers, but then divided the Formula into two so that the experiments could not be repeated. • Nathan and Tracy go to Mohinder for help, unaware of his mutation. • Noah orders Canfield to kill Sylar, but he refuses and disappears into a vortex. Sylar warns Claire not to trust Noah. • A villain called Eric Doyle has trapped Meredith and is controlling her every move. • Angela wakes up paralyzed after a disturbing dream. • At Pinehearst, Daphne has been hired by Linderman to recruit people, including Matt. She realizes that Linderman is not real. When she leaves, Maury emerges. He is later seen talking telepathically with the man from Angela's dream, who is on a life support system. The man is Arthur Petrelli.

DYING OF THE LIGHT

EPISODE 3.6 Daphne briefs Hiro to find Usutu. When she leaves, Ando gets up; his death was faked. • Knox places Adam Monroe's hand in Arthur's. As Adam turns to dust Arthur sits up in bed, fully recovered. • Matt returns from Africa, and Daphne tries to recruit him. • Mohinder drugs and binds Nathan and Tracy. • At Primatech, Daphne frees Sylar but he refuses to join Pinehearst and she leaves. Sylar then releases Peter, and they visit Angela. Peter looks into her mind and draws the helix, which Sylar recognizes from the Pinehearst business card. Arguing over Angela, Peter fights with Sylar, and leaves him tied up in a cell. • Hiro sees Usutu's paintings of Arthur, the villains, and the helix. • Sandra and Claire are captured by Doyle and made to play Russian roulette with Meredith, but Claire knocks out Eric. Noah invites Meredith to become a partner in the Company. • Daphne goes to recruit Mohinder, but after seeing Nathan and Tracy entrapped, she returns to Matt. • Tracy freezes Mohinder's hand, breaks her straps, and releases Nathan. • At Pinehearst, Peter is astonished to see his father. Arthur asks his son for a hug and drains his powers.

ERIS QUOD SUM

EPISODE 3.7 Leaving Nathan and Tracy in the lab, Mohinder takes Maya from her cocoon and flies her to Pinehearst to ask Arthur Petrelli to cure her. Arthur does this by stripping her powers and taking them for himself. After Maya leaves, Arthur offers Mohinder a chance to work at his lab. Mohinder agrees, in the hope of finding a cure for his mutation. • Elle comes to the Bennet house looking for Noah. She wants help because she is no longer able to control her powers. Claire agrees to travel with her to Pinehearst to find out what is going on. On the plane, Elle's powers nearly cause a crash but Claire intervenes. • After dreaming of Angela telling him he is her favorite son and asking him to save Peter, Sylar manages to free himself. He goes to Pinehearst, and finds Mohinder is preparing to experiment on Peter. While Sylar and Mohinder fight, Peter escapes. Arthur breaks up the fight, acknowledging Sylar as his son. • Arthur orders Daphne to shoot Matt for refusing to be recruited as a villain. Maury protests, reminding Arthur that he only agreed to help on condition that nothing would happen to Matt, but Arthur kills him by breaking his neck. Daphne goes to Matt's apartment but is unable to go through with the killing when Matt reminds her of his vision of the future in which they are married. Knox comes after Matt and Daphne, but Matt casts an illusion to get rid of him, making him think they are both dead. Daphne later calls Arthur to let him know she has got Matt's trust; she is still working as a double agent. • Arthur tries to turn Sylar against Angela, saying that she tried to drown him when he was a baby. When Peter returns, there is a fight and Sylar throws him out of the window. Peter lands, seemingly unhurt despite being without his powers, and just as Claire and Elle arrive. He warns them not to go in, but Elle does so anyway, determined to get help with controlling her powers. • Claire calls Nathan to say Arthur is back. Peter warns Nathan it is too dangerous to challenge Arthur. He pretends to agree, but secretly decides to go to see him anyway. • In Africa, Hiro is reluctant to go back in time as Usutu wants. But he accepts a paste offered to him by Usutu and collapses, his eyes turning white.

VILLAINS

EPISODE 3.8 This episode shows the three visions that Hiro has while under the influence of Usutu's drug. • In the first vision, Hiro travels back 18 months in time and sees Arthur and Linderman planning the car crash that was meant to kill Nathan and put an end to his investigations. • Horrified when she realises that Arthur is trying to plant the idea in her brain that Nathan must die, Angela poisons him. She thinks she has succeeded in killing him, but really he is only paralysed. • Hiro then travels to Memphis a year ago, where Meredith is recruited to be an agent of the Company, but later frees herself and her brother Flint from their clutches. • In a third vision Hiro sees Sylar, as Gabriel Gray, make a suicide attempt after his first murder. He is befriended by Elle, who has been asked to bring him in by Noah and the Company. Elle sees that Sylar seems to be trying to control his hunger to kill, and argues with Noah that they should help him. But Noah demands that she provoke Sylar so that they can witness his ability to kill and absorb powers. Noah provides a victim—a man called Trevor, who can cause spontaneous explosions—and eventually Sylar succumbs to the urge to kill. • Hiro awakens from his trance to find Usutu has been beheaded. Beside him stands Arthur Petrelli.

IT'S COMING

EPISODE 3.9 Hiro teleports himself and Ando to safety, but becomes stuck with the mind of a ten year old. In the latest copy of *9th Wonders!* he sees a picture of an eclipse, with a speech bubble reading "It's coming…". • Placed in a Pinehearst exam room with an angry Elle, Sylar finds that for the first time he is able to acquire someone's powers without killing them, and they bond. • At Pinehearst, Arthur asks Nathan to accept recent events as part of his destiny. Confused, Nathan decides to go to see Angela. • Tracy goes to Arthur, offering to persuade Nathan to cooperate in return for help with her career. • At the Pinehearst lab, Mohinder's experiments are having horrifying results. He feels that the serum is missing a catalyst. • Peter and Claire narrowly escape from Knox and Flint. As they run through a familiar alley, Peter is reminded of the Future Claire who shoots him. • At Primatech, Angela lies in a coma. Matt enters a nightmare in her mind in which she has been shackled by Arthur, but she manages to take control and makes him release her. Matt comes round from the dream as Angela also wakes. • When Peter, Claire, and Nathan arrive, Angela reveals that there is a third part of the Formula; a human blood Catalyst. Claire realises that it must be her, remembering how Sylar saw something "different" in her brain. • Arthur Petrelli, in a trance, draws five prophetic images. The last shows Noah holding a dying Claire in his arms.

THE ECLIPSE, PART 1

EPISODE 3.10 As a new eclipse approaches, Mohinder emerges, fully recovered, from a deep sleep in a self-woven cocoon. • At the same time, others begin to lose their abilities. • Nathan and Peter are flying over Haiti where they have come to ask the Haitian to remove Arthur's abilities. As Nathan's power fails, they fall out of the sky into the jungle, where a the Haitian's brother, a villain named Baron Samedi, captures Nathan. • Panicking about double-crossing Matt, Daphne flees to her home in Kansas. Matt, Hiro, and Ando follow her. She hides inside the house, and Matt finds he cannot read her thoughts. • Sylar and Elle go to the Canfield house where Claire and Noah are hiding out. Elle is unable to zap Claire, and Sylar's powers don't work either. In the confusion, shots are fired. Claire takes a bullet for Noah but is unable to regenerate. • Arthur and Flint demand that Mohinder gets their abilities back. • Matt shouts to Daphne inside the house. She lets him in, and he sees that without her powers she has cerebral palsy, and wears arm and leg braces. • Tracy calls Arthur, and is told that she must go to Parris Island, the Marine training facility. Afterwards, she realises Angela may have overheard. • At the Bennet house, Claire's wound becomes infected and she is very sick. • Elle and Sylar ponder on what happened to their powers. As they kiss, atop a nearby building Noah aims a rifle at them.

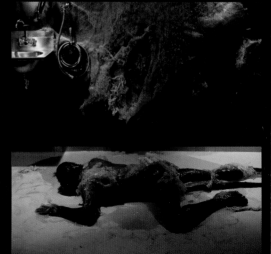

THE ECLIPSE, PART 2

EPISODE 3.11 The eclipse is still darkening the sky. • Mohinder escapes from Pinehearst. • Noah shoots at Sylar and Elle as they run from him. When he catches up with them, he cuts Sylar's throat and leaves him for dead while Elle remains hidden in an elevator. • In a comic shop, Hiro, still stuck with the mind of a ten year old, and Ando buy back issues of *9th Wonders!*, looking for clues. • Peter and the Haitian catch Samedi off guard as he assaults one of a pair of captive Haitian sisters. They temporarily overpower him and release Nathan and the girls from their shackles. As Samedi's militia come running, Peter takes a gun and turns to face them, giving the others time to run. • In hospital, Claire goes into septic shock and dies. • The eclipse finally passes, and people's abilities begin to return. • Claire regenerates and flees the hospital with Sandra. • Matt and Daphne both recover their powers, and after talking through their doubts, they embrace. • As Samedi's men are about to take down Peter the Haitian returns and wipes their minds. Peter, Nathan, and the Haitian combine their now recovered powers to defeat Samedi. • As Mohinder is on his way to visit Maya, he relapses to his mutated form, his scales reappearing. He goes back to work for Pinehearst. • In the comic shop, Hiro teleports away, appearing at the Bennet house as a recovered Sylar prepares to kill Noah. Hiro grabs Sylar and Elle, then returns for Claire. • Nathan decides that the right people need to be given powers, to make the world a better place. He tells Peter he is going to Pinehearst. • The comic shop manager reveals that Isaac Mendez gave a sketchbook to a bicycle messenger. • Hiro teleports Claire to the rooftop of the Deveaux building where she sees herself as a baby being handed over to Noah. • Left in Costa Verde with Elle, Sylar reverts to his old self and slices open Elle's skull.

OUR FATHER

EPISODE 3.12 After traveling back in time with Hiro, Claire witnesses events on the Deveaux rooftop 16 years in the past. She becomes convinced that if she can stop the Company from transferring the Catalyst to her infant self, Arthur Petrelli's plan will never happen. She succeeds in preventing Noah from handing baby Claire back to Kaito to receive the Catalyst, but instead it is transferred into the 10 year old Hiro by its current host, his dying mother, Ishi. • Arthur follows Claire to the past looking for the Catalyst, but finds it is not in her. Instead, he detects it in Hiro when he arrives to save Claire. Arthur strips the Catalyst from Hiro, then throws him from the Deveaux rooftop. • At Primatech, Claire tells Noah, Angela, and Meredith the bad news that Arthur now has all three parts of the Formula. • Nathan allies himself with Arthur and finds that Tracy is already working for Pinehearst • Now that Arthur has the Catalyst, the Formula is complete. Nathan and Tracy watch the Formula being tried out on a volunteer soldier, with great success. Mohinder is confident it will cure his own mutations • Peter understands that he must kill Arthur, but regrets having to do it and wishes there was another way. • After burning Elle's body in Costa Verde, Sylar resumes his hunt for the people on Chandra Suresh's List. He kills an office worker named Sparrow Redhouse and steals her lie detector powers. He then hunts down Arthur. Sylar finds Arthur just as he is being confronted by the Haitian and a wavering Peter. Using his new power, Sylar learns that Arthur is not really his father, and kills him before Peter can. • Ando, Matt, and Daphne track down the bike messenger who has Isaac's sketchbook. Inside they find the draft of the last edition of *9th Wonders!* They see a sketch of Hiro being thrown off the Deveaux building rooftop by Arthur, and decide that their only chance of saving him is to try to get the ability to time travel from Arthur and give it to Ando.

WAR

EPISODE 3.13 Knox and Flint turn on Nathan, who they think has lied to them. They help Peter destroy the paper Formula, angering Nathan who hoped it could be used for the good of humankind. • Tracy leaves Nathan when he refuses to run from the situation with her. • Matt, Ando, and Daphne look for Mohinder hoping to get the Formula from him. • Sylar goes after Angela. Noah, Meredith, and Angela don't believe there is any way to stop him, but Claire knows that it is possible to shut down his brain by obstructing a sweet spot at the back of the head. • Mohinder is held at gunpoint by Peter when Daphne appears in a blur of speed and steals a syringe containing the Formula. • A vat of Formula falls on Mohinder, and his scales disappear—he is cured • When it looks like Knox will kill Nathan, Peter injects himself with the Formula to gain the power to save him. • Claire uses a shard of glass to stab Sylar in the head and prevent him from using his powers, and he is trapped inside Primatech as the building explodes. Mohinder also seemingly dies in the explosion • Hiro is stuck in the past, stripped of his powers. Ando injects himself with the Formula and gains the ability to supercharge Daphne's speed to the point where she is faster than time. They race back in time and rescue Hiro, then come back and destroy the Formula, at least in its paper form. • After the Primatech explosion, Peter tells Nathan that he has lost: the Formula is gone and the world is safe. Nathan is still convinced the Formula could have been used to help humankind. He responds to Peter's betrayal by confessing his powers to the US President, and outing the Heroes.

CLEAR AND PRESENT DANGER

EPISODE 3.14 Nathan begins sending out masked teams of "hunters" to round up people with special powers. Tracy and Mohinder are both brought in. • As the hunters abduct a woman named Denise, Sylar appears and slaughters them all, then kills Denise and takes her powers. Nathan learns from his chief Hunter that somebody has taken out an entire team. • At Yamagato Industries' New York division, Hiro and Ando quarrel and Ando speeds off on his new "Ando-cycle". Later, over a comms-link, he hears Hiro being abducted and tracks him to an airport. • Matt is confronted at home by Usutu and Isaac Mendez, who tell him he must paint the future. • Peter and Nathan agree to meet for dinner and clear the air, but as Peter gets ready the hunters arrive and take him in. • Snooping in Nathan's office, Claire discovers Angela and Nathan plan to take out Matt Parkman. She goes to his apartment, and as she and Matt discuss his trance drawing, the hunters burst in and capture them both. • At the airstrip, Tracy, Matt, Peter, Mohinder, and Hiro are put onto a plane, shackled and drugged. As Claire is led towards the plane, Nathan offers her a chance to lead a normal life if she will stop interfering. She agrees and leaves, but returns and slips aboard the plane just in time for take off. • In the cabin, Claire releases Peter, who holds the guards at bay while Claire rushes to the cockpit. She is stunned to see the co-pilot is Noah. • While struggling with the guards, Peter absorbs Tracy's power and accidentally freezes the plane, causing it to crack. A huge hole opens up, and the plane plummets towards the ground.

GLOSSARY

A

ACTIVATING EVOLUTION
A book written by geneticist Chandra Suresh, explaining his theories about human evolution and the emergence of extraordinary powers.

ADOPTIVE MUSCLE MEMORY
The ability to replicate any observed physical act.

ALCHEMY
The ability to turn metals into gold using touch.

ALGORITHM, THE
A formula, devised by Chandra Suresh, to pinpoint the location of evolved humans.

B

BLOOD RECIPIENTS
People who have received blood from others whose blood has extraordinary healing properties.

BUTTERFLY EFFECT, THE
The act of changing one past event, which then has repercussions on much larger events, completely changing the outcome of history.

C

CATALYST, THE
The mysterious factor that enables the Formula to work, carried in the blood of an individual. Sometimes the carrier him/herself is referred to as the Catalyst.

CLAIRVOYANCE
The ability of a person to watch people or events that are happening far away.

COMPANY, THE
A secret, illicit organization, founded in 1977, that seeks to find evolved humans, and track, lock up, or eliminate them depending on the level of danger they are thought to present. The Company has its own scientists and doctors as well as agents who track the activities of suspicious individuals.

CYBERPATHY
The ability to communicate with digital data.

D

DEVEAUX BUILDING, THE
A building in New York owned by Charles Deveaux. Its rooftop has been the scene of many important events.

DEPARTMENT OF HOMELAND SECURITY
A federal agency in the USA. It is responsible for responding to natural disasters as well as protecting the country from terrorist attacks.

E

ECLIPSE
The passing of the moon between the Sun and the Earth, causing the sky to darken temporarily. Solar eclipses appear to be linked to the emergence and disappearance of evolved abilities.

ELECTRICAL MANIPULATION
The ability to generate and emit electrical energy.

EMPATHIC MIMICRY
The ability to absorb the special powers of others and to reproduce these powers at future times by mentally visualising the source individual.

EVOLVED HUMANS
People with genetically mutated or chemically manipulated genes which give them special abilities.

F

FORMULA, THE
A formula developed by the Company to endow people with synthetic special abilities.

FREEZING
The ability to freeze any substance.

G

GENESIS FILES
A series of files compiled by Chandra Suresh about the powers of various evolved people.

GROUP OF TWELVE, THE
The twelve founder members of the Company. They are Susan Amman, Daniel Linderman, Arthur Petrelli, Angela Petrelli, Kaito Nakamura, Victoria Pratt, Bob Bishop, Maury Parkman, Paula Gramble, Charles Deveaux, Carlos Mendez, and Harry Fletcher.

H

HELIX SYMBOL, THE
A recurring Symbol linked to evolved humans. It is believed to represent human DNA, a Japanese character, and the Haitian myth of the serpent who swallowed a crane. Some of the places it appears are: Chandra Suresh's algorithm, the cover of *9th Wonders!*, Isaac's and Usutu's paintings, Jessica's tattoo, Adam's death threats, Molly's drawings, Takezo Kensei's sword, and the Pinehearst logo.

HEALING
The ability to cure people, animals, and plants through touch, short of reviving the dead.

HUMAN GENOME PROJECT
A scientific project whose purpose was to identify all the genes in human DNA. The 13-year project, a combined effort by scientists from the USA, the UK, Japan, France, Germany, and others, ended in 2003.

"HUNGER," THE
A term used by Sylar to describe his overwhelming urge to kill others with special abilities and absorb their powers for himself.

I

ILLUSION
The ability to create false perceptions of reality in order to deceive others.

INDUCED RADIOACTIVITY
The ability to emit lethal levels of ionizing radiation.

INTUITIVE APTITUDE
The ability to understand and replicate how any organic or mechanical system works, including how the brain manifests special abilities. However it is accompanied by the "hunger" (see above).

INVISIBILITY
The ability of a person to move amongst others without being seen.

K

KIRBY PLAZA
A building complex in New York, where the Company has a facility with labs and offices.

L

LEVEL 2/LEVEL 5
Secure prison facilities at Primatech Research where the Company holds people who they believe to be dangerous. The prisoners on Level 2 are considered less of a threat than those on Level 5.

LINDERMAN GROUP, THE
An umbrella organisation headed by Daniel Linderman which operates mafia-like criminal activities under the cover of a business empire in the hotel/gambling industry.

LIST, THE
A list compiled by Chandra Suresh naming 36 people suspected of being evolved humans. In Mohinder's possession after Chandra's death, the List was later stolen by Sylar.

LOCATIONAL CLAIRVOYANCE
The ability to locate any living person anywhere.

M

MARK, THE
A mark, looking like two small slits, that is seen on the necks of evolved humans examined by the Company. It is made by a pneumatic syringe, which injects an isotope marker for tracking purposes.

MAP, THE
A map on which Chandra Suresh pinned photos of evolved humans and linked them with strings.

MEMORY REMOVAL
The ability to wipe memories from others' minds.

MOSAIC FILE, THE
A file in Mohinder Suresh's possession with data about Peter Petrelli's ability to replicate the abilities of others by altering his genetic structure.

N

9TH WONDERS!
A comic book written, drawn, and published by Isaac Mendez. It shows, in comic strip form, events in Hiro Nakamura's life that have not yet happened.

P

PATIENT ZERO
Sylar was Patient Zero—the first person Chandra Suresh found who could prove his theories.

PHARMATECH INDUSTRIAL
The makers of the pneumatic syringes used by the Company to inject tracking markers into people.

PHASING
The ability of a person to pass all or part of their body through solid objects.

PINEHEARST COMPANY
A biotech research company set up by Arthur Petrelli. Its aim is to use biotechnology to create armies of super-powered people.

POISON EMISSION
An ability that causes someone to emit a deadly substance whenever he or she is scared or stressed.

POWER ABSORPTION
The ability of a person to drain the special powers of another, absorbing them for their own use and leaving the source person powerless.

POWER DAMPENING
The ability to block special powers.

PRECOGNITION
The ability to see events in the future through various means, including dreaming or painting.

PRIMATECH PAPER COMPANY
A paper production and distribution company in Odessa, Texas, that functions as a front for the activities of the Company. The Primatech warehouses, factories and offices conceal secret medical facilities and cells for prisoners.

PRIMATECH RESEARCH
A facility owned by the Company in Hartsdale, NY, containing offices, labs, training facilities, medical facilities, prisons, a gymnasium, and a library.

PUPPETMASTER
A person with the ability to control others' physical actions by moving his arms.

PYROKINESIS
The ability to generate and control fire.

R

RAPID CELLULAR REGENERATION
The ability to regenerate cells, thereby healing any damage to the body almost instantly.

S

SHANTI VIRUS, THE
A potentially deadly virus that affects the nervous system and blocks the powers of evolved humans. It was named after its first known victim, Mohinder Suresh's elder sister Shanti.

SPACE/TIME MANIPULATION
The ability to bend the space-time continuum and fold it to move instantly from one place to another or backwards or forwards in time.

STRING MAP
Models made using interconnecting pieces of string that represent paths through time. Used by both Hiro Nakamura and Peter Petrelli to identify the key moment to change the course of history.

T

TAKEZO KENSEI
A Samurai Warrior of Japanese legend. Recorded as a brave and honorable figure, his exploits include success at the Battle of 12 Swords and the Battle of 90 Angry Ronin, saving the swordsmith, and falling for his daughter. In reality, these were carried out by both Adam Monroe and Hiro Nakamura.

TECHNOPATHY
The ability to manipulate electrical equipment.

TELEKINESIS
The ability to move objects using only the mind.

TELEPATHY
The ability by which a person connects their mind to the mind of another, enabling them to read and send thoughts, or search for memories.

TRACKING
The practice of monitoring the movements of suspicious individuals. The Company has used two systems: the Walker Tracking System (see below) and isotope markers traced by a satellite.

W

WALKER TRACKING SYSTEM
A name given to Molly Walker by the Company when they are using her to locate people.

V

VOCAL PERSUASION
The ability to control people's actions by giving them verbal instructions.

Y

YAMAGATO INDUSTRIES
A Tokyo-based company founded by Kaito Nakamura that employs Hiro Nakamura and Ando Masahashi as computer programmers.

INDEX

Figures in bold indicate illustrations

HEROES REVEALED

LONDON, NEW YORK, MUNICH,
MELBOURNE AND DELHI

Designed by Dan Bunyan for DK Publishing

Project Editor Elizabeth Dowsett
Managing Editor Catherine Saunders
Art Director Lisa Lanzarini
Publishing Manager Simon Beecroft
Category Publisher Alex Allan
Production Editor Clare McLean
Production Controller Nick Seston

First published in the United States in 2009
by DK Publishing
375 Hudson Street, New York, New York 10014

09 10 11 12 13   10 9 8 7 6 5 4 3 2 1
HD150—02/09

DK books are available at special discounts when purchased in bulk for sales promotions, premiums, fund-raising,
or educational use. For details, contact:
DK Publishing Special Markets, 375 Hudson Street, New York, New York 10014, SpecialSales@dk.com.

A catalog record for this book is available from the Library of Congress.

ISBN: 978-0-7566-4116-0

Color reproduction by MDP in the UK
Printed and bound in China by L-Rex

ACKNOWLEDGMENTS

The author would like gratefully to thank:

Tim Kring, the entire team at *Heroes*, and NBC for creating this amazing story, and entrusting me to take an
extended look inside it so that I could tell the rest of the world what I found.

Simon Beecroft at DK for kindly remembering how much I enjoy doing this stuff and DK's Elizabeth Dowsett
for being a true collaborator and a first-rate editor.

I also want to thank my beloved wife, Bari, for staying in good humor while I took this on (again).

And most importantly, I'd like to dedicate my effort on this project to the two great Heroes of my life—Jake Berger
Goldman and Nathan Berger Goldman.

The publisher would like to thank Neysa Gordon, Steve Coulter, Mitch Steele, Kim Niemi, and Leslie Schwartz
at NBC Universal. Thanks also go to Julia March for the episode summaries, the glossary, and for proofreading